Gently and tenderly he reached for her hand

Meg blushed, feeling a disproportionate pleasure in his simple touch. She looked at his well-kept, tanned and ringless hand, which gave an impression of his latent strength. The warmth from his skin seemed to burn into her flesh, and she felt oddly breathless. Knowing she had to break the contact, she brushed the hair from her face.

"Stop running," Paul drawled lazily, moving closer. "What are you afraid of, Meg?"

"You," Meg could have said. But instead she replied, "Nothing. I don't like being touched, that's all."

"You're quite wrong, you know," he whispered. "You like it very much. So much, in fact, you're frightened by my touch...and by me."

SANDRA FIELD

walk by my side

Harlequin Books

TORONTO • NEW YORK • LOS ANGELES • LONDON
AMSTERDAM • PARIS • SYDNEY • HAMBURG
STOCKHOLM • ATHENS • TOKYO • MILAN

Harlequin Presents first edition February 1983
ISBN 0-373-10568-1

Original hardcover edition published in 1982
by Mills & Boon Limited

CHAPTER ONE

'ARE we nearly there?' Chris muttered fretfully.

'I'm not sure,' Paul replied, keeping his voice matter-of-fact. 'I think I may have taken a wrong turn a while back. Why don't you try and go to sleep again, Chris? I'll wake you as soon as we arrive.'

The boy made an indeterminate reply, curling up against his pillow on the opposite side of the car seat, as far away from his father as he could get. With a pang of the mingled tenderness and pain that Chris seemed always to arouse in him, Paul glanced over at the little boy, wishing that the child trusted him enough to cuddle up to him. He would have liked Chris's head to have been leaning against his jacket rather than against the car door, he would have liked to be able to put his arm around the boy as they drove together through the rain-swept darkness. He stifled a sharp sigh, wondering if that day would ever come. It would take time for Chris to learn to trust him, the psychiatrist at the hospital had said. Time and patience . . .

Paul had plenty of both. What he had not realised back in those early days at the hospital was how much his son's continued rejection of him would hurt. He loved the boy; but Chris had made it painfully clear he did not want that love.

Deliberately Paul wrenched his thoughts away from Chris, for it was ground he had covered a hundred times, and there were no easy answers. If, indeed, any answers at all. At least, he noticed abstractedly as he peered through the windshield, the child had fallen asleep again; he must be worn out . . . and that, of course, was just what the doctors had warned against. In a small gesture that bespoke an agony of frustration, Paul's palm hit the steering wheel, for once again he was thinking about Chris.

As for the predicament they found themselves in now, he, Paul, had no one to blame but himself. Their plane had been delayed in leaving Toronto: a bomb scare that had necessitated a complete search of the plane from one end to the other. So they had been late arriving in Halifax. Then there had been a mix-up in his car rental that had taken a further half hour to straighten out. What he should have done then was to drive straight to Halifax and stay in a hotel there, thereby making sure that Chris had a good night's sleep. But Chris had wanted to get 'to the sea', and he himself had been anxious to leave the cities behind. So he had phoned the guest house where they had reservations and had received a very complicated series of directions from Rose Huntingdon, its proprietor, whom he pictured, perhaps unfairly, as a fluttery, wispy-haired spinster. 'It's really very simple, Mr Moreton,' she had assured him. 'You can't possibly get lost.'

Well, he had certainly proved her wrong, Paul Moreton thought grimly, turning the wipers to the highest speed. He had absolutely no idea where he was, or even in what direction he was heading. About ten miles back he had turned left at the bridge, as she had suggested, and then there had been a complicated series of forks in the road, where he had more or less blindly followed his instincts. He should have known better. A year and a half ago he had followed his instincts, believing himself to be on the verge of the most explosive news story of his career, and he had ended up in a foreign jail for eleven long months. Which was, he recognised wryly, yet another unproductive line of thought.

In front of him the road divided again, this time into two far narrower tracks, each of which disappeared into the darkness. There was no signpost. He hadn't seen one for five miles. He took the right-hand fork, discovering that the road wound circuitously through a landscape that seemed to be all rock, only a few shrubs alleviating its harshness; to his left the headlights swept over a gleam of water. A lake? A cove? Surely he had glimpsed seaweed?

He drove on, forcing himself to concentrate on the unfamiliar road, in his ears the drumming of rain on the roof and the rhythmic sweep of the wipers, and beneath all that, the tiny flutter of his son's breathing. The first house he saw, he decided, he must stop and ask directions, even if that risked waking Chris up again; he couldn't keep driving like this indefinitely. As if his decision had conjured them up, when he topped the next rise he saw far to his right the twinkle of lights—a village of some sort. Did this road veer round to it? Or should he have headed in that direction some way back? Then, in front of him, the car lights picked out two houses near the edge of the road, each with a truck parked in the driveway—and each in total darkness.

Paul glanced at the illuminated dial of his wristwatch. Ten-thirty. Perhaps they were fishermen, who had to be up before dawn. Which didn't help him at all right now. Still, there were bound to be other houses, and surely not everyone would be in bed by now. Down a dip, round another rise, again the illusive gleam of water. Downhill, then up between two weathered buildings that looked like fish shacks. With an abruptness that made him jam on the brakes the road widened into an area of solid rock that then dropped off into the sea.

Breathing a little faster than normal, Paul sat very still behind the wheel, silently giving thanks that he had not been driving any faster. There was more to give thanks for, he realised, for ahead of him across the water shone a single light from a rectangular window. All he had to do now was hope they had a phone.

'Where are we? Are we there?' Chris had struggled upright, rubbing at his eyes with his fists.

'We're somewhere, certainly,' Paul said drily. 'I'm going to go to that house and see if I can use their phone, or at least try and get directions back to Bayfield, where we're supposed to be staying. You stay here, okay? I won't be a minute.'

'I'm coming with you,' Chris announced, his eyes darting nervously around at the black night.

'Chris, it's pouring with rain——'

'I don't want to stay by myself.' The boy's lower lip quivered.

Paul could hardly blame him, for there was something about the place that felt like the very end of the world. 'All right,' he capitulated, reaching over into the back seat for Chris's yellow raincoat. 'Here, put this on and pull up the hood.' He himself had only a light jacket—he'd just have to get wet. He got the flashlight out of the dash. 'Ready? Stay put and I'll come round and get you.'

He got out of the car and immediately distinguished three new sounds: the slap of water on the rocks below and the more distant thunder of ocean waves against the shoreline, both overlaid by the keening of the wind. They had arrived at the sea, that much was certain. He went around the hood of the Pontiac and opened Chris's door. 'Want me to carry you?'

'No, thanks,' was the polite reply, a reply Paul supposed he could have anticipated.

'Take my hand, then. I don't want to lose you,' said Paul, not altogether joking.

He shone the beam of the flashlight ahead of them and heard the first sounds of animation in the boy's voice as Chris cried, 'It's an island! Look—there's a little bridge.'

To their left the ground sloped more gradually downwards, a path beaten in the grass. Across a fifteen-foot divide, where the black waters surged back and forth, a narrow wooden bridge had been built, with railings on either side; it rested on piled-up rocks on each shore. Chris tugged at Paul's hand, apparently oblivious of the wind and the rain. 'Let's go across it.'

Bending his head against the rain, which had already soaked his hair and face, Paul allowed himself to be led across the bridge and up the opposite slope to the more level ground. There were three houses, he saw, two of them in darkness. The third seemed to be little more than a fish shack, its shingles unpainted, its peaked roof covered in tar paper. Yet there was a wooden ramp leading to the door and curtains at the two front windows, and behind the curtains the welcome glow of light. He walked up the ramp, raised his hand and knocked on the door.

The sound made Meg jump. Who on earth could it be at

this hour of the night? It certainly wasn't her grandfather, who had a special tap all of his own. Nor would it be Ada, for she was usually in bed by ten.

During the three months Meg had been here on the island, there had been the slow flowering of a sense of security; it was a totally new way of life after all the years she had spent in Vancouver, the people as different as day from night. Because her father was a very wealthy man, the owner of a twenty-one-room house on spacious, beautifully landscaped grounds, they had always lived hedged in by security: they had a burglar alarm system connected to the nearest police station; all the doors were locked and bolted at night; a Dobermann Pinscher roamed the grounds. All this to protect the art collection, the antique furniture and imported carpets that her father deemed the necessary prerequisites of a man of his status. In all fairness, he was right to insist on burglar alarms and double locks, since Vancouver had one of the highest crime rates in the country. Unlike Cairns Island. In consequence, Meg realised now, as once again there came a sharp tap at the door, she had not bothered to latch the door, and whoever was out there had only to turn the handle.

She *was* on Cairns Island, she thought stoutly, not in Vancouver. No harm could come to her here. Raising her voice, she called out, 'Come in!'

A hesitation, then the handle turned and the door opened. A child was the first to enter, a boy of four or five, she judged, in a wet yellow rain slicker. The man who followed, his dark hair plastered to his forehead, was undoubtedly the boy's father, for they had identical brown eyes, so deep a brown as to be almost black. The man pulled the door shut behind him and looked over at her.

By now she should be used to that startled lowering of the gaze to her level, but even yet it could make her inwardly flinch. Unconsciously she raised her chin. She had been sitting directly in the light, her embroidery frame in her lap, the silks a tangle of bright colours on the table beside her. Some of the light was caught in her hair, which fell honey-gold to her shoulders; her eyes were a

clear, direct blue in a face fined down to reveal its exquisite bone structure, its high cheekbones, and wide forehead.

The silence had stretched on long enough, and she said
with quiet dignity, 'Can I help you?'

The man was still staring at her, his face very pale, his
eyes blank with shock. She saw him rake his hands
through his wet hair, but before he could speak, the little
boy had taken the initiative. 'How come you're in a
wheelchair?' he asked.

Almost she was grateful for his directness. 'Because I
can't walk,' she said evenly.

'Why not?' the boy asked. His father made a restraining
gesture, which the child ignored.

'I had—an accident.'

'Were you in hospital?'

'Yes, I was.'

'So was I—I hated it!'

If anyone had said to her five minutes ago she would
be having this kind of a conversation with a small boy
who was a complete stranger, she would have told them
they were crazy. Yet as the boy spoke, she sensed a change
in the tall man standing in the shadows behind him: a
sharpening of attention, a focussing, that more than words
told her the conversation was important. She asked
casually, 'Why were you in hospital?'

The child had walked across the floor to stand within
two feet of her. He looked as though he had been ill, she
thought; there was no colour in his cheeks and his face
was far too thin. 'I had an op'ration.'

'I see.'

'Did they hurt you when you were in the hospital?'

'Chris——'

With a tiny movement of her hand, she silenced the
man. What the child wanted to say was more important
than any notions of politeness or convention. 'Yes, they
did sometimes, Chris,' she said, glad to know his name.

'Me, too. I hated it,' he repeated fiercely.

She said carefully, 'I think they have to hurt you sometimes to try and make you better.'

He spoke with the absence of artifice that is the mark of the very young. 'But they didn't make *you* better.'

In spite of herself, she winced. 'No. They can't do everything, Chris. They're only human, after all.'

'Will you ever be able to walk again?'

Since she had moved here there had been talk of the possibility of an operation, but the odds against success seemed too great, and the illusory hope it raised too painful for her to contemplate. 'I don't think so,' she replied.

Something must have shown in her face, for the man said heavily, 'That's enough, Chris. I'm sorry, Miss—I don't even know your name.'

'Please don't apologise. And my name is Meg Cairns.'

'I'm Paul Moreton. My son, Chris.'

For the first time since they had arrived, she smiled, a smile that gave her face the warmth of true beauty. 'Do come in, Mr Moreton,' she urged. 'You'd better come by the fire, you're soaked.'

As he walked farther into the room he gave a quick glance around, and she wondered what he thought of his surroundings. Many years ago the building had been a fishing shack; since then her grandfather had scoured it clean of the smell of bait and dried fish, and insulated it and had electricity brought in. On the plain board walls she had hung three of her favourite paintings, while figured cotton curtains on the windows added more colour. Because of her wheelchair there were no rugs on the worn pine floors. The furniture was very simple: a wooden table and chairs, a sink with kitchen counter and cupboards, a small electric stove and refrigerator. A door led into the bathroom. Against the wall that overlooked the water was a three-quarter bed, covered with a scarlet spread and a red and white quilt, and nearby a dresser and wardrobe. The centre of the room was taken up by an airtight wood stove, which threw a comforting heat; the woodbox beside it was heaped with neatly split logs and kindling—again the work of her grandfather.

Paul Moreton had come into the circle of light, gratefully holding out his hands to the warmth. 'We're lost,' he said in a voice whose attractively deep timbre she had already noticed. 'We came here because yours was the only place to show a light.'

'We came across the bridge,' Chris piped.

She laughed. 'It's only half an island really, Chris. At high tide you have to use the bridge, but at low tide you can jump across the rocks.'

'That sounds like fun,' he said wistfully. 'Tomorrow morning will it be low tide?'

She made some quick calculations. 'Not until after lunch, I guess.'

'If we stayed here, we could see it.' From under long dark lashes the boy looked up at his father.

'Of course we can't stay, Chris,' he said sharply. 'We'll get directions from Miss Cairns——'

'Meg, please,' she interrupted.

'—and then we must leave,' he went on, disregarding her. 'We're going to be very late as it is.'

He was a man used to being obeyed, Meg thought shrewdly, noticing Chris's crestfallen look. 'Where were you going?' she asked.

'A bed-and-breakfast place in Bayfield.'

'Bayfield!' she echoed. 'Goodness, that's twenty miles east of here. You must have taken the wrong turn-off quite a way back.'

With some asperity he remarked, 'As there weren't any signposts, that wouldn't be difficult.'

'The roads here are really only used by the local people—fortunately the tourists haven't discovered the place. Hence no signposts.'

'Where are we, anyway?'

'On Cairns Island—my grandfather owns it. The village of Heron Cove is on another peninsula farther to the west.'

'That would be the lights I saw . . . is there a motel there?'

'In Heron Cove?' She laughed. 'Heavens, no! I told you it hadn't been discovered by the tourists.'

His frustration was palpable. 'In that case we'll have to try and find Bayfield.'

She made an instant decision, one that would have

horrified her cautious, security-minded father. 'Don't worry about it,' she said. 'You can both stay here.'

Chris's, 'Yeah—let's!' and Paul Moreton's, 'We can't possibly do that,' were spoken together. The man's voice overrode the boy's. 'Chris, we can't stay here. We've only just met Miss Cairns for one thing, and for another the lady at the guest house is expecting us.'

Meg's grandfather would have recognised the danger signal as the girl's hands tightened on the padded arms of her chair. 'First of all, my name is Meg,' she said roundly. 'And secondly, I don't issue invitations I don't mean.'

'I'm sure your invitation was very kindly meant,' the man replied. 'However, if you'll just give us directions to Bayfield, we'll be on our way.'

'I don't think I can. There's a maze of backroads between here and there and I'm quite sure I'd get you lost again. So unless you want to spend the night driving along every little bay and inlet along the coast, you'd better stay here.' And put that in your pipe and smoke it, she thought childishly.

He changed tactics. 'I can only see one bed,' he said smoothly. 'While it might be big enough for you and Chris, it would hardly take the three of us.'

She could no more have stopped the blush that flooded her cheeks than she could have stopped breathing. 'There's a room upstairs,' she seethed, losing all restraint. 'I, of course, can't possibly get up there. But the two of you can. Unless you find the idea of being in the same house with someone who's a cripple utterly repugnant.'

His eyes narrowed. 'You know damn well I don't feel that way.'

She felt at once exhilarated by their verbal battle and horrified at herself for being so rude. 'Good,' she said. 'Then that's settled, isn't it?'

'You win round one,' was the dry response. 'Don't expect to win the second one, will you?'

'I don't think you're used to being the loser,' she guessed shrewdly.

'It makes an interesting change.' Something in the man's big body relaxed infinitesimally. 'Now that we've got that over with, may I ask if you make a habit of inviting complete strangers to stay with you?'

A dimple appeared in each cheek. 'Not at all,' she said demurely. 'But then it's not very often that complete strangers arrive on my doorstep at this time of night.'

He grinned suddenly. 'You're very persuasive.'

He had not smiled before; it changed his whole demeanour from a somewhat formidable reserve to a far more relaxed and more youthful friendliness. But before she could say anything—and the change in him had been startling enough that she would have been searching for words—Chris, who had been following this dialogue without comprehension, said plaintively, 'Are we staying?'

'Yes,' his father replied, 'and it's high time you were in bed, young man. I'll go and get our suitcases out of the car.'

'And I'll make some cocoa,' Meg said briskly. 'Chris, do you like chocolate chip cookies?'

When Paul Moreton came back a few minutes later, Meg was just pouring three mugs of steaming cocoa, and there was a plate of cookies on the table as well. She wheeled herself back and forth between the table and the sink with an absentminded efficiency that was obviously second nature to her; her grandfather had rearranged all the cupboards and shelves to be at her level. As they drank the cocoa, Chris asked, 'How do we get upstairs, Meg?'

'There's a ladder—your father will have to put it in place.' While Chris's solemn little face lit up at the prospect of climbing to bed on a ladder, Meg added, 'This building used to be a fish shack, you see, Chris. So it's built on stilts out over the rocks, and from the window upstairs you can look right down into the water. There's a double bed up there—I hope you'll both be comfortable.' She flicked a light switch and above them there was illuminated a square hole in the ceiling.

Paul got up and unhooked the wooden ladder from the wall, fixing it in place in the grooves provided. With an easy strength he swung each suitcase up into the room. 'I'm glad there's a railing around the hole,' he remarked.

'Wouldn't want Chris falling down it.'

'It's quite safe. There's even a barricade to go across the gap.'

It took ten or fifteen minutes to get Chris settled for bed. He had to climb upstairs and get into his pyjamas, come back down to use the bathroom and get a drink, and then go up again, plainly entranced by the whole procedure. After getting his drink, he paused by Meg's chair. 'G'night, Meg,' he said shyly. 'I'm glad we're staying.'

'I'm glad you are, too,' she said. 'Sleep well.'

He clambered up the ladder and she heard the low murmur of Paul Moreton's voice, then his, 'Goodnight, Chris.' A pause before Chris's response, which even from downstairs she could tell was only lukewarm. 'N'Night.' Not, 'Goodnight, Dad.' In fact, she thought, her mind running back over the past hour, she had not yet heard Chris call his father anything. Yet Paul Moreton must be his father, the physical resemblance was too great for the relationship to be otherwise.

Paul himself had just jumped to the floor and she gazed at him uncertainly, her perplexity clearly to be read in her face. Without stopping to think, she said in a low voice, 'He *is* your son, isn't he?'

'Oh yes, he's my son.'

'But——'

'Beyond that, may I suggest you mind your own business?'

An edge of steel in the silken voice. Once again taken off guard, Meg flushed angrily. 'I beg your pardon,' she snapped. 'I like him and I was interested, that's all.'

He passed a hand across his forehead and sat down heavily in one of the chairs. 'I'm sorry——that was quite uncalled for. The trouble is, it's a sensitive subject.' As if to make amends, he went on, 'Chris likes you, too——that's obvious. It's the first real interest I've seen him show since——well, since a long time.'

Picking her words with care, she said, 'In that case, I'm glad you stayed.' He was sitting with his head down-bent, his fingers——which were long and beautifully shaped, she noticed—absently playing with his cocoa mug. The light shone obliquely over his face, gleaming in the thick dark hair, throwing into relief the strong line of his jaw, the harshly carved profile; his eyes, dark and unfathomable, were gazing sightlessly at the table. It was not a happy face, she thought, for there was pain and struggle in the lines that ran from cheek to mouth. It was an intensely private face; he would not easily share with anyone the memory of that pain, the frustration of the struggle.

He glanced up to find her gazing at him and it was his turn to look at her. She was wearing a pure white peasant blouse with an embroidered neckline and a pale blue wool skirt, its gathered folds revealing slender ankles and high-arched feet, and she bore his scrutiny with a poise beyond her years. 'How old are you?' he demanded abruptly.

'Twenty-two. And you?'

He gave a bark of laughter. 'You do say what's on your mind, don't you? Fair enough. I'm thirty-five. Who else lives on the island, Meg?'

It was the first time he had called her by name; ridiculously she knew she liked it. 'My grandfather, Ben Cairns, lives in the white house. Ada MacKinnon, who's a widow, lives in the other house.'

'Your parents are dead?'

'Oh, no, they live in Vancouver.'

'So why are you here? Did you grow up here?'

'You know,' she said slowly, 'I could tell *you* to mind *your* own business.'

Brown eyes met blue, clashed and held. 'You could indeed. But you won't.'

Her temper was rising. 'Give me one good reason why not.'

'Because I want to know about you, Meg Cairns. I want to know why a beautiful young woman like you is living in a fish shack miles from anywhere. I want to know what—or who—you're hiding from.'

'I'm not hiding from anything. Or anyone.'

'No? Then why are you here?'

She picked up her embroidery frame and stabbed the needle through the cloth, the silk a brilliant green against the white fabric. Normally she thought of herself as an even-tempered girl. So what was it about this man that seemed to arouse instant antagonism? Before she could formulate a reply, he was speaking again, this time with a sincerity that disarmed her. 'I really would like to know, Meg.'

She looked up, her expression troubled. 'I've never met anyone quite like you before,' she blurted. Nor had she. He could not in any way be compared to Kevin. And as for the men who had crowded her life before the accident, Philip included, he made them seem in retrospect like young boys, crass and immature in their endless search for fun and excitement. He was older, of course. But it was more than that. Already she sensed an innate maturity and strength that must have been forged over a lifetime.

'That could be mutual,' he said softly, and for a moment his eyes lingered on the vulnerable curve of her mouth.

It was almost as though he had touched her. Danger, her nerve ends screamed, and instinctively she shrank back in the chair. 'I don't want to tell you,' she said breathlessly. 'I've never yet made a habit of pouring out my life story to comparative strangers, and I don't see why I should start with you.'

She saw his jawline tighten and waited apprehensively for an explosion of anger. Instead he said emotionlessly, 'You'll change your mind before I leave—I guarantee you that.'

'Mr Moreton, you'll be gone in the morning.'

'Oh? Is that an order or a request?' he drawled.

'You're certainly not staying here more than one night!'

'Be very careful—I never could resist a dare.'

'This is a crazy conversation,' she stormed, her needlework forgotten in her lap. 'An hour ago you couldn't wait to get out of here.'

'True. But I always think one should be capable of—

er—flexibility, don't you, Meg?'

She felt a thoroughly juvenile urge to poke her tongue out at him, and then, when he began to laugh, knew he had read her intention as clearly as if she had done it. But before she could say anything, he had stood up. 'I think it's time we called it quits.' He yawned widely. 'Besides which, I'm ready for bed. One way or another it's been quite a day. Is there anything I can do for you, Meg, before I go up?'

'No, thank you. I can manage fine on my own.'

'You're a very independent lady, I'm beginning to realise.' One hand on the ladder, he added, 'Do you never get lonely here, Meg?'

She was surprised into honesty. 'Yes, sometimes I do. But never as lonely as I was back in Vancouver when I was surrounded by people.'

'So you know about that kind of loneliness, too . . . Goodnight, Meg.'

'Goodnight, Paul.'

As she got ready for bed she heard the faint sounds from overhead as he moved around, then finally the snap of the light switch and the creak of the bed springs. She finished washing, then lowered herself out of her chair into bed, turning off the bedside light right away. Quite often she would read for a while before sleeping, but tonight she knew the book would not hold her attention. She lay still, gazing into the darkness, hearing the rain-drops hit the windowpane, and the waves splash and gurgle around the rocks. Familiar sounds, both of them. Why then did she have the feeling that everything had changed?

CHAPTER TWO

MEG woke early the next morning to an obscure feeling of excitement that somehow today was different. And so it was, she recollected swiftly. For she had visitors, Paul and Chris. They would be leaving this morning, she supposed, to continue on their journey, only then realising that she had no idea where they were from or where they were going. She would probably never know . . . and after all, why should it matter? She should be glad that she had been able to help them . . .

Too restless to stay in bed any longer, she sat on the edge of the bed and swung herself into her wheelchair. After going to the bathroom, she chose a pink wool dress from her cupboard, knowing it became her, and brushed her hair until it crackled with a life of its own. She smoothed a matching lipstick on her mouth, and put on tiny gold earrings. There was still only silence from overhead, so she quietly let herself out of the door, wheeling her chair up the ramp and stopping in the flat open area of grass to take in a deep breath of the early morning air.

It was going to be a beautiful day. The sky was a clear pale blue, rinsed clean by the night's rain. A crisp spring breeze tugged at her hair and made the fishing boats rock on their moorings in the cove. Ben's bright green one, the *Harriet III*. The two white Cape Islanders belonging to Ada's sons. Dave Robert's gold-painted boat with its matching dory turning in slow circles on its line. A group of gulls were perched on the opposite shore, their plumage a startling white against the grey rocks and dark green spruce trees.

She might have been early, but Ben was up ahead of her. He had been carrying kindling into his back porch, and now he brushed the wood chips off his much-darned grey sweater as he strode across the grass towards her. 'Morning, Meg.'

'Hello, Grandpa.' She smiled affectionately into the blue eyes that were very like her own, although from his radiated out the lines of a man who had spent much of his life outdoors. His hair and beard were grizzled, his skin perpetually tanned; nearing seventy, he could still haul his lobster traps, cut all his own wood, and look after a garden.

'Car parked over there, I see. Wonder whose it is?'

It was Paul's, of course, a dark blue sedan. 'I had visitors last night,' she explained. 'A man and his son who were looking for Bayfield and had got lost.'

'They wouldn't be the first to do that, now. You mean they stayed over?'

'That's right. They wanted me to give them directions, but I really couldn't.'

'A sense of direction's not one of your strong points, lass.'

It was a long-standing joke between them, for Meg regularly got confused even going into Camden, the nearest town. 'I know! Oh, look, here comes Chris now.'

She waved as the little boy came across the ramp, 'Hi, Chris! Chris, I'd like you to meet my grandfather, Mr Cairns. Grandpa, this is Chris Moreton.'

'Call me Ben,' the older man said gruffly, his calloused hand engulfing Chris's tiny one. 'I likely wouldn't answer if you called me Mr Cairns—wouldn't know who you meant. And where are you from, young feller?'

'Toronto,' Chris said promptly. 'But we're going to spend the summer in Nova Scotia.'

'Are you now? And have you been by the sea before?'

The wind tousled the boy's dark hair. 'We went to Spain once and that was by the sea. But it wasn't nearly as nice as this. Is the tide down yet?'

'Not for a few hours yet. When it's down you can find starfish and crabs in the rock pools.'

The little boy eyed Meg anxiously. 'Do you think my father will let me stay that long?'

She thought it was very unlikely, but she hated to dash his hopes. 'I don't know, Chris. Maybe we should go down and start some breakfast—is he awake yet?'

'I'm not sure.' Nor did he sound very interested, the

girl thought ruefully, again aware of the chasm that seemed to stretch between son and father.

Ben said cheerfully, 'Tell you what, Chris—while Meg cooks breakfast, you come and help me stack kindling, and I'll tell you about the time I got my boat hung up on Gull Rocks. You see that reef out there beyond the light-house?' He pointed down the cove towards the open sea.

Chris's eyes lit up. 'Okay. Was it a shipwreck?'

The two of them disappeared around the back of Ben's house, the boy's hand tucked confidently in Ben's. Meg smiled to herself. That would be the last she'd see of Chris for a while, for she knew all too well how Ben's stories could enthrall young imaginations. And not so young, either. She herself had spent more than one evening at Ben's, listening to him tell of his adventures as a young man on the swordfishing boats, or as a seaman on a cor-vette in the war.

Carefully she navigated the slope down to the fish shack and pushed open the door. There was the sound of splashing water in the bathroom, and as she shut the door behind her, Paul emerged, rubbing his face and neck on a towel. 'Morning, Meg,' he said cheerfully.

He was naked to the waist. A mat of dark hair extended from neck to navel, and he was powerfully built, broad-shouldered and deep-chested. Suddenly aware that she was staring at him as if she'd never seen a man before, she stammered, 'Oh—good morning. Did you sleep well?'

'Great! Where's Chris?'

'Up with my grandfather. I came to make breakfast.'

'I'll get shaved, then.'

He went back into the bathroom and she could hear him whistling as he turned on the tap again. It was a commonplace enough action, she supposed, yet under the circumstances it had a peculiar intimacy. Giving herself a mental shake, she started the bacon frying and put the coffee percolator on before laying the table.

By some built-in radar system perhaps common to all small boys, Chris arrived just as Meg was putting the breakfast on the table. He burst unceremoniously in the door, not seeing his father at first. 'Meg, Ben's going to take me out in the dory after breakfast—he wants to get some stuff off his boat. Mackerel jiggers, to put new feathers on them. He says I can help. Can I hurry up and eat so I can go back out?'

She chuckled. 'Everything's ready, so tuck right in.' He looked very different this morning than he had last night when he arrived, she thought. The wind had brought some colour to his cheeks and his eyes were bright with anticipation.

'Morning, son,' said Paul, as he pulled up a chair at the table and passed Meg the bacon.

For a moment the animation died from Chris's face. 'Morning,' he mumbled through a mouthful of toast.

Paul made no visible reaction, his hand perfectly steady as he held the plate out to Meg. Yet the girl knew instinctively that he was hurt, and her smile was perhaps warmer than she intended as she said, 'Thank you, Paul. Help yourself to the scrambled eggs. Chris, if you're going out in the boat, you'd better put on an extra sweater, it's always colder on the water.'

'Okay.' He crammed another piece of toast in his mouth.

'Your grandfather still goes out fishing, does he?' Paul asked Meg.

'Every chance he gets,' she replied, and began telling him about the various types of fishing done in the area, very much aware of Chris listening wide-eyed to every word. They finished eating and Chris said, wriggling impatiently in his chair, 'May I be excused, please?', obviously a formula he had been taught.

'Clean your teeth,' said Paul. 'Have you taken your pill?'

'No.' The sulky look was back on Chris's face.

'They're in my shaving kit in the bathroom. Would you bring them here, please?'

Chris stomped off to the bathroom, perfunctorily cleaned his teeth, then came back with the pill container. Paul took one of the small green capsules and gave it to the boy, who swallowed it down with a mouthful of milk. 'Now can I go?' Chris demanded.

'Remember what the doctor said about too much running, okay? Have a good time.' Paul reached out to tousle his son's head, but somehow the boy evaded the gesture and was out of the door.

'Why can't he run too much, Paul?' Meg asked, risking once again being told to mind her own business.

'He had open-heart surgery and he still has to be a bit careful. Trouble is, I don't want to be over-protective and smother the kid in warnings—don't do this and don't do that.'

'What about the future? Will he be able to do anything he wants?'

'The operation was a complete success—we were very fortunate in that respect.'

'We', she thought uneasily. That little word must not only encompass Paul and Chris, but Chris's mother as well—and where was she now? Her pleasure in having been able to offer hospitality to these chance-met strangers suddenly evaporated; yet she was honest enough with herself to admit that it had been a pleasure. They had brought a breath of the outside world with them, a new interest. She was curious to know more about them: why Chris avoided his father; why they had come to the south shore; what Paul did for a living and what made him tick. She pushed her chair back from the table, avoiding Paul's eyes. It was a good thing they would be leaving today. She had fought too hard for the serenity she had achieved over the past couple of months to want it disrupted by two people who could mean nothing to her in the long run. Once they were gone, her life would settle back into its peaceful, repetitive groove.

That it was not to be so, she was soon to find out. After she and Paul had cleaned up the breakfast dishes, restricting their conversation to impersonal subjects by a kind of mutual consent, they both went outdoors. From behind Ada's house, with its neat green shutters and window-boxes, drifted the sound of voices, and as they approached they saw Ben Cairns holding a basket of wet clothes for a slender white-haired woman who was hanging them on the line. The sheets were flapping in the breeze like sails,

while a row of socks performed a lively dance. Chris was
holding the bag of clothes pegs. 'That's Ada with Ben, my
grandfather,' Meg said in explanation. 'Let's go and say
hello.'

By the time they got there, Ada had just clipped on the
last garment, and she turned to smile a welcome at them.
Her hair was the first thing you noticed about her, for it
was the pure white of the sheets behind her, thick and
luxuriant; she wore it in a loose bun on the back of her
head. Her face, with its faded blue eyes and wrinkled
cheeks, still bore a vestige of the beauty that many years
ago had had all the young fishermen from Camden to
South Point tramping to her father's doorstep. The second
thing you noticed was the twinkle in her eye; she had not
escaped tragedy and sadness in her sixty-five years, but
neither had she let them quench her zest for living. Her
beloved Jonathan, who had been her husband for more
than thirty years, as well as Ben's best friend, had died
ten years ago; but she had six children scattered in the
villages along the coast, and fifteen grandchildren, and
there was nothing she liked better than to have them all
crowding into her little house so that she could feed them
vast quantities of food and catch up on all the family
gossip.

Now she called, 'Good morning! Hello, Meg. And you
must be Chris's father—I'm Ada MacKinnon.'

'And I'm Ben Cairns,' Ben offered.

They shook hands and chatted for a few minutes, then
Paul said, 'Maybe you can help me, Mrs MacKinnon.
I'm looking for a place where my son and I can board for
the summer. Somewhere by the sea, preferably. I want it
quiet enough that I can do some writing, yet it needs to
be the kind of place where Chris can spend a lot of time
outdoors. Would you know of anywhere suitable in the
area?'

Ada tilted her head to one side, her shrewd eyes making
a lightning assessment of the tall, dark-haired man standing beside Meg's wheelchair. 'Well now, I know of one
place,' she said brightly. 'How about right here? I'd love
to have a couple of boarders, I never have been able to

get used to cooking for one person. You could use the back parlour for your writing. And there's four bedrooms upstairs—you could each have your own room.'

'That sounds ideal,' said Paul with suspicious prompt-ness, and Meg was visited with the conviction that he had hoped Ada would offer her house. 'Would you mind if I looked at the rooms right now, and we could discuss terms?'

'Come right in,' Ada urged. 'I might even find Chris a molasses cookie.'

'You mean we'd stay here all summer?' Chris inter-rupted breathlessly.

'Would you like that?' Paul asked.

'And live next door to Ben and Meg?' Paul nodded. 'Yeah, I'd like that!'

'Let's go inside and see if we can settle it, then. Maybe you can choose which bedroom you'd like.'

The three of them disappeared and Ben looked over at his granddaughter. 'That was quick work,' he commented drily.

Meg felt as though the smile was pasted on her face, for Paul had given her no inkling of his intentions. But then why should he? she argued inwardly. He was free to stay wherever he pleased, wasn't he? She didn't own the island, after all. She was only here herself because of her grand-father's generosity.

'Yes, it was, wasn't it?' She glanced up at Ben, re-cognising the glum look on his face. It was no secret that for the past five years Ben had been trying to persuade Ada to marry him and that she would have nothing to do with his plan. Two boarders wouldn't help Ben at all. They would only keep Ada busier than usual so that she would have even less time for her next door neighbour. 'It's too bad, Grandpa.'

'Ah, well, she likes to be busy,' he grunted. 'And it'll make a change, I suppose. Bit of new life on the island.' He cheered up visibly. 'It'll be nice to have the boy around, for sure.'

Meg's heart went out to him, for she heard the loneli-ness in the gruff voice. Ben's wife had died twenty years ago; his only child was her father, who had chosen to make his life as far from Cairns Island as possible, on the opposite coast of the country. She herself was an only child, and now she would certainly never marry and fill Ben's house with great-grandchildren.

'He seems a nice little boy,' she ventured. 'Although there's something wrong between him and his father.'

'You noticed that too, eh? The lad never mentions his father if he can help it—strange. Ah, here they come.'

Chris came running across the grass. 'We're going to stay,' he crowed. 'I'll be able to find the starfishes at low tide and walk across the rocks where the bridge is.'

Paul's eyes went straight to the girl in the pink dress. As if speaking to her alone, he said, 'Everything's settled. I'll move our cases out of your place and up to Ada's. But in the meantime I have to go into Halifax and pick up our trunk at the station.' He glanced over at his son. 'Would you like to come, Chris?'

Before they boy could answer, Ben interjected, 'I believe the two of us have some work to do on the boat—I'll keep an eye on him for you while you're gone.'

'In that case I'm sure Meg will come with me. We can go right now.'

'I'm not——' Meg began crossly.

'That's a grand idea,' said Ben. 'Meg doesn't get much chance to get off the island—it'd be good for her.'

'And don't you worry about a thing, dear,' Ada added briskly. 'I'll look after your supper this evening.'

'Great,' said Paul before the girl could even think of an excuse. He came behind her chair, let off the brake and turned it around. 'We might as well leave right away. We can have lunch at the hotel.'

In a simmering silence Meg allowed herself to be wheeled down the hill and across the bridge. Only when they had reached Paul's car and she knew she was out of earshot of Ben and Ada did she say furiously, 'Look, Paul Moreton, this has gone far enough——'

'I am looking,' he said cheerfully. 'A very pretty picture you make. Your cheeks are the same colour as your dress—being in a temper suits you.'

'Oh!' she exploded. 'Take me back over the bridge this minute. I don't want to go with you.'

He leaned against the car and folded his arms, with the air of a man who has all the time in the world. 'Why not?'

'To start with, you manipulated that whole thing, suggesting it in front of Ben and Ada, when you knew darn well they'd approve.'

Amusement gleamed in his eyes. 'Right on.'

'You never even *asked* me if I wanted to go!'

'There wasn't much point—I was almost sure you'd say no.'

'You were absolutely right,' she stormed. 'So now you can take me back. And don't worry, I'll think of something to tell Ben and Ada so we won't sully your lily-white image.'

'You have a mean tongue in you,' he said appreciatively. 'I like a woman who can stick up for herself.'

Was there no way she could puncture his self-possession? She heard herself say shrewishly, 'Talking of women, I presume Chris must have a mother—where is she?'

He drew a breath in a sharp hiss and she saw the first signs of anger in his face. 'I would imagine she's in Monaco with her doting husband. That's where she goes every year at this time. What else would you like to know?'

She shrank back in her chair, for his voice had been cutting. 'I—I'm sorry. I shouldn't have asked that.'

'No, you shouldn't.' He opened the car door on the passenger side and bent to adjust the footrests on the wheelchair.

'What are you doing?'

'I'm going to put you in the car so we can go to Halifax.'

'I don't want to go!'

Still stooping, he looked up at her, his brown eyes relentless. 'I really don't care whether you want to go or not, Meg—you're going.'

Her hands were gripping the arms of her chair so that

the skin was stretched taut across the knuckles. 'Make me,' she said rebelliously.

'Oh, that's easy.' In one smooth motion he slid his arms around her and picked her up out of the chair.

Her face with its startled blue eyes was only a foot from his, because automatically she had linked her arms around his neck when he had picked her up. She had a confused impression of solidity and warmth and strength; of a man's body too close for comfort; and, so evasive that it almost escaped her, an impression of utter security. Fighting for breath, she demanded, 'Put me down—I'm far too heavy.'

'I rather like it.'

Horrified by her own reactions, she knew that she did, too, and it was this that made her protest all the louder. 'Please, Paul—put me down!'

He was wearing an open shirt under a V-necked pull-over, and she could see the heavy beat of the pulse at the base of his neck. For a moment that filled her with a wild, sweet excitement quite unlike anything she had ever felt before, she thought he was going to kiss her. But then he shifted her slightly in his arms, his expression altering subtly, and with a mixture of disappointment and relief, she knew he had changed his mind. Instead he edged the wheelchair out of the way with his foot and lowered her into the car seat, reaching across her to buckle the seat-belt. Not until he had straightened and slammed the car door did she let out her pent-up breath in a long sigh.

He folded the wheelchair and lifted it into the trunk, then came around to the driver's side, got in, and started the car. As he reversed over the rocks, she could think of absolutely nothing to say. She need not have worried.

'How long since you've been to Halifax?'

'A month,' she said stiffly.

'Who dragooned you into going then?'

'I had a doctor's appointment.'

'Oh?' Briefly he rested his hand on her knee. 'Stop sulking because you didn't get your own way, Meg, and tell me what happened that caused you to end up in a wheelchair.'

'I'm not sulking!' she retorted. Then, her native honesty getting the better of her, 'Well, maybe I am—a bit. Did anyone ever tell you you're rude, inconsiderate, and over-bearing?'

'I'm only that way with someone who doesn't do what he—or she—is told.'

'There's no reason in the world why I should have to do one thing you want me to do.'

'Yes, there is. Because right now you're having fun, aren't you, Meg?'

She stared at him, horrified. It was true, of course—she *had* been enjoying their verbal fencing. She had felt fully alive, her brain working with a peculiar clarity. Suddenly terrified, she said incoherently, 'Paul, there's no point in us . . . that is, I can't be . . .' She scarcely knew what she wanted to say. She only knew she felt threatened, desperately unsure of herself.

'What are you getting at, Meg? Right or left here, by the way?'

'Left. I don't know . . . only that . . .' Again she stumbled to a halt.

'Are you saying we can't be friends? Is that it?'

'I—maybe.'

'Why not?'

'Because I'm a cripple!' The ugly words burst out.

'I thought that might be it. Left here again, I presume?' He negotiated the turn smoothly. 'You know as well as I do that that's quite the wrong word to use in connection with you. There's nothing wrong with your brains. You're sensitive and kind, I can tell that already. And on top of all that, you're a very beautiful woman. Any number of men would be delighted to have you as a friend.'

'That's not true! I had dozens of friends before the accident. When I came home two months afterwards, they'd all dropped out of sight. They didn't want to be bothered with me once I couldn't ride or dance or ski. I wasn't any fun any more.' Some of the pain of that abandonment was still in her voice.

'Then they were not true friends to start with,' he said implacably. 'Very few people are lucky enough to have "dozens" of friends, anyway.'

'Even those I thought were close friends didn't stay around.' To this day she had never mentioned the pain of Philip's desertion to another living soul, and what she had just said was as close as she could get to it.

She missed his lightning-swift glance in her direction. 'Tell me about the accident,' he said patiently. 'Were you skiing?'

'No, we were riding, cross-country. A friend of mine and I.' It had been Philip, of course. 'We had a bet on to see who could get to the top of the hill first. I was determined to win, so I risked jumping the stream at its widest point, because that was the most direct route. My horse—he was a big black gelding—stumbled and fell, I fell off, and the horse rolled on my legs.' She shivered. 'At least, that's what they told me happened. Luckily I was knocked out, so I remember very little.'

'How long were you in hospital?'

'Nearly two months. Then I was home for three months before my grandfather invited me to come to Cairns Island. Thank goodness—I was nearly going out of my mind at home.'

His thoughts were still obviously on the accident. 'I somehow can't quite picture you taking a bet like that.'

'Oh, I was different in those days. I've had time to do a lot of thinking since then—even some belated growing up.' Her laugh had an edge of bitterness to it. 'As they say in the psychology magazines, it was a learning experience.'

'Life can deal us plenty of those,' he responded soberly. 'It just depends what you do with them, doesn't it? Meg, is there no chance of improvement for you?'

Her fingers pleated the material of her skirt, her hair hiding her face. 'I don't think so. Oh, the specialist in Halifax when I first went there three months ago talked of the possibility of an operation, but he was very vague, and the odds against success were quite high. He hasn't mentioned it since.' Refusing to sound self-pitying, she

added, 'I don't mind as much now. I seem to have come
to terms with it, more or less.'

'You're a very brave woman.'

She blushed, feeling a disproportionate pleasure in his
simple words, perhaps because she sensed he was not a
man to hand out praise that he did not mean. While
speaking he had removed one hand from the steering
wheel and had placed it over hers. It was a well-kept
hand, ringless, tanned, giving an impression of latent
strength. The warmth from his skin seemed to burn into
her flesh and she felt oddly breathless. Knowing she had
to break the contact, she made the pretence of pushing
her hair back from her face.

'Stop running, Meg,' he said lazily.

'What do you mean?'

'You reacted as if I was about to make an improper
advance just then. What are you scared of?'

'You', she could have said. 'Nothing. I don't like being
touched, that's all.'

'You're quite wrong, you know. You like it very much.
So much that you're afraid of it.'

'If you know the answer, why do you bother asking the
question?'

'I wanted to get it out in the open . . . this looks like
the turn-off for the main highway, is it?'

'Yes.' As he drove along the ramp she said sharply, 'I
wish you'd stop making that kind of remark. I feel as
though you're playing games with me all the time.'

He slowed down at the yield sign and checked the
mirror for traffic before pulling on to the highway. 'That's
not true, Meg. All I'm trying to do is make you more self-
aware. And I'm absolutely sincere when I say I would
like to be your friend.'

She was silent, too confused by all the contradictory
effects he had on her to know what to reply.

'We're going to be spending the summer together on
the island, right? Pretty close quarters, you must admit.
So it's logical we should be friends. You and Chris hit it
off from the start, and there's no reason why you and I
can't do the same.'

No logical reason. No rational reason. Only the quivering of her nerve ends warning her of danger, the reaction of her body counselling her to beware. It had taken her eight long months to reach the comparative senenity that characterised her life now . . . she could not afford to let one man disrupt it. But she had one more weapon left. She said coolly, 'Has it not occurred to you that I might not be a suitable friend for either you or your son?'

'No, I can't say it has.'

'You obviously never read the gossip columns. I even made it to a couple of national magazines if you missed the Vancouver papers.'

'Oh . . . what for?' His query indicated merely a polite level of interest.

'Just about everything you can think about. Wild parties. Champagne breakfasts. Affairs with any number of men. Too much of everything—money, drink, clothes, men—you name it.'

If she had hoped to shock him, she was disappointed. Instead he laughed outright. 'How on earth did I miss all that?'

'Don't you believe me?' Her voice rose in annoyance.

'Now that you mention it, I think I have seen a picture of you somewhere. Did you go by the name of Margaret Cairns, rather than Meg?' She nodded. 'Then I have. You were looking quite astonishly voluptuous in a long silver gown with only a minimal amount of bodice to it. As I recall, the man with you—was it Philip somebody or other?—looked drunk. You merely looked—underneath all the glitter and a considerable amount of make-up— quite desperately unhappy.'

In a flash of insight she accused him heatedly, 'You're not just remembering that now—you've known it all along.'

'Mmm . . . I was wondering if you'd see fit to reveal the secrets of your wicked and dissipated past to me.'

'Oh, do stop talking like a second-rate villain! I don't think I've ever met anyone quite as aggravating as you.'

'Well, that's a start, I suppose.'

'Anyway, you'd surely agree that makes me an unfit companion for your son?'

He spoke with quiet intensity. 'Let's stop fooling each other, Meg. For whatever reason, you made an instant impression on Chris. You know that as well as I do. He'd never spoken to me or to anyone else about his experiences in hospital, but he did to you. He needs that kind of an outlet, and I'm asking you to provide it for him, to be his friend. And I'm asking you to let me be your friend as well.'

She was shaken by the depth of emotion behind his words. Shaken and disarmed. For she knew what he had said was true. There had been an instant affinity between her and Chris, and she perhaps could meet Chris's needs in a way no one else had been able to. His mother had remarried and was on the other side of the world, and he was estranged from his father—whom else did he have? With a sense that she was stepping into the unknown, she said quietly, 'All right—I'll do my best with him.' Farther than that she could not go.

'Thanks, Meg.'

No effusive gratitude. No outpouring of emotion. And no reference to the fact that she had not promised to be *his* friend. So perhaps she was still safe . . .

As if he had had enough of the subject, he began telling her about an exhibition of Maritime artists he had seen in Toronto, and from there the conversation moved to books and music. Before Meg knew it they were driving through the busy streets of the city and then Paul was parking in front of the railway station. 'Won't be a minute,' he said. It was five minutes before he was back with a porter, a brown leather trunk on the cart. They eased it into the back seat, Paul tipped the man and then came around to Meg's window. 'We might as well park right here—we're near enough to the hotel.'

'Paul, couldn't we go home for lunch?'

'Why, Meg?'

There was no point in prevaricating; he'd find out the truth about her sooner or later. 'I don't enjoy eating in restaurants. I always feel so selfconscious.'

When her grandfather brought her in to Halifax to the doctor's, he was as anxious as she to get straight back to

Cairns Island. Her parents, in the two months she had
been at home, had never taken her anywhere; she was an
embarrassment to them, she knew—nice girls didn't end
up in wheelchairs. So her public appearances, as she
ironically dubbed them, had been limited to the nightmare journey from the west coast to the east, during which
she had spent the whole time imagining that everyone
was staring at her, pitying her, whispering behind her
back.

'Selfconscious? Nonsense. All the women will be envying your looks and all the men will be envying me.
Nothing to it.'

He knew as well as she did that it was not that simple.
Equally he was going to insist on her going. 'Lend me a
comb, then,' she said in a resigned voice as he helped her
into the wheelchair. 'As you virtually dragged me off in
the car, I didn't even have the chance to get my handbag.'
Her mouth quirked. 'At least this way you know who's
going to pay for lunch!'

He chuckled, wheeling her across the pavement. 'You'd
better pick the most expensive thing on the menu by way
of revenge.'

'Chateaubriand and champagne.'

'What a hell of a combination—can't you do better
than that?'

They were both laughing as the doorman ushered them
into the lobby. She said decorously, 'I'm waiting to see
the prices on the wine list—then I'll decide.'

'Exploited again!' he groaned.

'Not only that, but it's all your own fault.'

The restaurant was dimly lit, and fairly busy; there was
a subdued hum of conversation. As the hostess led them
across to their table, no one appeared to pay much attention to them. The waiter swiftly removed the extra chair
and then the menus were in front of them and Paul was
consulting her about her preference in cocktails. Slowly
Meg began to relax. It seemed a very long time since she
had been in a place like this; and, she thought wryly, in
those days more often than not she had been the one to
pay the bill. Philip had always been punctilious in paying

his own share, it was one of the things she had liked about
him; but many of her other friends had been only too
glad to let the wealthy Margaret Cairns look after the
bill. Paul was right, she realised that now—they had not
been true friends. Hangers-on would be a better word.
And because she had always craved people and noise and
activity she had allowed herself to be used . . .

'Penny for them.'

She started. 'Oh—sorry.' After a moment's hesitation
she went on, 'I think what you said earlier was quite
true—my so-called friends were not true friends.
Acquaintances, perhaps. But not friends.'

'A very definite distinction. Which reminds me—you've
said you'll be Chris's friend, but you haven't said you'll
be mine.'

She had the sense that something momentous was about
to happen, something that would alter her life irrevocably.
There was no way she could avoid his level brown gaze,
nowhere she could run and hide, even if she wanted to.

She had to make a decision. Turn her back on this man
and opt for the calm day-to-day existence that she had so
painstakingly constructed after her accident, with its small
pleasures and correspondingly small disappointments. Or
take the risk of breaking the pattern, allowing Paul to
become a part of her life with all the changes that would
incur. Look what he had done already, in less than
twenty-four hours . . . The new Meg of the past three
months, patient and quiet and very much in control,
would choose the former path, and protect what she had
built. But the old Margaret, whose frantic—and fruit-
less—search for something, or someone, of meaning, had
led her to take risk after risk, had never entirely been
subdued. Margaret had always taken the most dangerous
ski run in the iciest of conditions; danced all night and
gone swimming in the dawn. Margaret would have
welcomed the challenge of this handsome, dictatorial
stranger who yet seemed to know her as well as or better
than she knew herself . . .

Their cocktails had arrived and she raised her glass.
With an attempted lightness that did not quite succeed,

she said, 'To our friendship.'

His glass clinked against hers. 'To our friendship,' he repeated. Then, so matter-of-factly that it was pure anticlimax, he said, 'I think I'm going to try the lobster. What about you?'

She had scarcely glanced at the menu. 'The seafood crêpes,' she said, that being the first thing she noticed. 'And a salad.'

Throughout the meal he purposefully kept the conversation on a light plane, relating some amusing anecdotes from his past career, which she discovered was a mixture of traveller, political commentator, and journalist. In turn he drew from her, without her quite realising how it happened, a picture of her life before the accident: the vast house in which she and her mother and father had lived, cushioned from the realities of its upkeep by a company of servants; the formal dinners with all the right people; her mother's social life and her father's business concerns, which were so much more important than their child, who after all could be raised by the nannies and governesses they brought over from England.

They finished their meal and went back to the car, Meg too involved in describing her year in a French pension to notice whether or not people were paying any attention to them. When she finally finished her story, she said in faint surprise, 'I don't know what came over me—I don't usually talk this much.'

'Must have been the wine.'

It had not been the wine, she knew; it had been his obvious interest, his interposed questions, his apropos and often witty comments. Feeling suddenly selfconscious, and wishing she had not revealed quite so much about herself, she fell silent, watching the landscape slide past, a monotonous scenario of hills and rocks and trees. She leaned her head back against the seat, and in a few minutes her eyes closed.

CHAPTER THREE

IF Meg had expected every day to be like the first day that Paul and Chris had spent on the island, she was soon disillusioned. Paul's mention to Ada of doing some writing had not been casual small talk: he had meant every word of it. Four days passed during which Meg scarcely saw him, and it was from Chris that she learned Paul was setting up a work room at Ada's and was starting to 'get organised', to use Chris's words. In one sense it was re-assuring, for her vision of Paul turning her life upside down had obviously been an exaggeration. Yet at other times she was piqued at what seemed like avoidance of her. Was this all he had meant by friendship? Irritated at herself for even minding that a day could pass with-out her seeing him, she welcomed Chris's frequent visits. The boy's time seemed to be divided between her and Ben; with Ben he would help mend lobster traps and paint buoys and even cut up bait; with her he would read, play with his set of tin soldiers, and sometimes fall asleep on her couch during the hour or two he was supposed to rest every afternoon. She was spending more time than usual on her embroidery, perhaps because of his company, and the heap of finished articles was grow-ing at a satisfying rate—Kevin would be pleased, she knew.

Five days after Paul's arrival, a knock came at the door. It was late afternoon on a misty, grey day that had kept her indoors, so that company was doubly welcome. She called her usual, 'Come in!', wondering if it would be Paul. But when the door opened it was Kevin who came in, tiny beads of moisture on his reddish hair and beard, his work bag and guitar in his hand. Genuinely pleased to see him, she said warmly, 'Hi, Kevin. I hope you've brought me some new things, have you? I've nearly finished the last lot.'

'I sure have—even a couple of special orders.' He bent and kissed her cheek, leaving her skin damp. 'You look well, Meg. Nice to see you.'

Kevin Langley ran The Silver Tern, a craft shop in the nearby town of Camden, although he himself lived in Heron Cove. He was committed to maintaining the community of Heron Cove as an economically viable place to live and devoted a lot of his energy to encouraging the crafts of quilting, hooking rugs, embroidery, and knitting, selling the locally produced wares in his shop; he was also a potter in his own right. He insisted on one thing only: high quality workmanship. And he got it, for his gruff, low key manner concealed a rabid perfectionist who would not accept slipshod work. The reputation of his shop had spread far beyond Camden, and last summer he had done extremely well; this summer he expected to double his turnover. It was Ada who had first rekindled in Meg an old interest in embroidery, and who had then put Kevin in touch with her. He brought her tablecloths, place mats and centrepieces; at first from purchased stencils and then from her own designs, she embroidered them; he paid for her work, and then sold the articles in his shop.

They had known each other for nearly two months and Meg looked forward to his weekly visits; he had reached the point of confiding in her his problems with his girlfriend, Kathy, who lived in Halifax. She sounded far too flighty and fun-loving a girl for Kevin, and as far as Meg could see was leading him a merry dance. Kevin had many admirable attributes, but a sense of humour was not one of them.

'Let's see what you've done since my last visit,' he said now.

She spread out a bureau scarf of pale blue linen on which she had worked with satin stitch and stem stitch a design of interwoven flowers and leaves in subtle shades of blue and green; then a set of beige place mats each with an abstract border in rusts and browns; finally a table cloth of aqua-coloured fabric embroidered only in white, the colour of foam on the sea.

'Fantastic,' he said, examining the exquisitely aligned stitches with deep satisfaction. He unfolded another tablecloth which was splashed with all the vivid hues of the rainbow, his arm loosely across the back of her chair. 'That's a most interesting design—very effective.'

Behind them the door burst open and Chris came rushing in. 'Meg! Do you want to go out in the fishing boat with us?'

She turned her head, her hair falling loosely over Kevin's sleeve, and across the width of the room felt Paul's anger like a blow. Her fingers unconsciously creasing the crisp white folds of the tablecloth, she said, 'Hello, Paul. Hi, Chris. I don't think either of you have met Kevin, have you? Kevin Langley, Paul Moreton and his son, Chris.'

Kevin straightened, his slow, deliberate smile alleviating the squareness and stolidity his face had in repose. 'Hello, Paul. Chris. Nice to meet you both.'

'Hey, that's pretty,' said Chris. Then, suspiciously, to Kevin, 'Why are you looking at it? You don't do that kind of stuff, do you?'

'No,' Kevin said stiffly, seeing nothing remotely funny in the question.

Meg stifled a giggle, knowing how often in the past Kevin had had to defend his masculinity because of his occupation, even to the point of fisticuffs, although how anyone could think of him as the slightest bit feminine with his pugnacious chin and stocky build was beyond her. About to come to his rescue and explain his interest, she heard Paul ask, 'Are you nearly through, Meg? The fog's lifted quite a bit and we thought we'd go out in the boat for a while. Chris wants you to come.'

But you don't, she thought silently, noticing the tight-held mouth and stony eyes. She said coolly, 'I don't think it would be very sensible for me to go out in a boat, do you? Besides which, Kevin and I have quite a bit to do yet.'

'What sort of things?' Chris asked, his face falling.

'Kevin sells my needlework in his shop, Chris,' she explained. 'That way I can pay Ben for my light bills and food.'

'Your father must surely give you money?' Paul interjected sharply.

'Oh, yes, he gives me a monthly allowance. But don't you see, this way I'm independent. For the first time in my life I'm earning my own money, paying my own way. It's made such a difference to me, all the difference in the world.' On impulse she took Kevin's blunt-fingered hand and squeezed it briefly. 'I don't know how I can ever fully express my gratitude to Kevin.'

Kevin shifted uncomfortably, his cheeks flushed. 'Come off it, Meg. You do darn good work and you're getting paid for it. Don't make me into some kind of knight in shining armour.'

Sir Kevin Redbeard, she thought mischievously, knowing she could never share the joke with him. Before she could say anything more, Paul said abruptly, 'Come on, Chris, we'd better go. Goodbye, Kevin. We'll take you another time, Meg.'

'We'll see,' she temporised, knowing she had no intention of going with him. She didn't belong on the deck of a boat, not any more.

'That's right,' was the steely response. 'We will.' A curt nod in Kevin's direction and he left, Chris trailing behind him.

'Who's he?' Kevin asked without finesse, barely waiting until the door had shut.

She explained the circumstances of Paul's arrival, and the arrangement with Ada. 'So I guess they'll be on the island all summer,' she finished.

'He's a man who knows what he wants and goes after it—I wouldn't want to tangle with *him* on a dark night.'

She found she did not want to discuss Paul Moreton with Kevin or with anyone else. 'What did you bring me to work on?'

He brought over the bag of fabrics and threads and soon they were deep in discussion. Then Meg cooked supper for him, for this had become part of their routine. Because it was still overcast, dusk came early, and with it came Chris, who often spent an hour or two in the evenings curled up on Meg's couch, reading. By now Kevin had his guitar out, tuning it, and Chris watched in silent fascination as Kevin plucked the strings, adjusting each peg until he had the pitch he desired. Then, his blunt, square-nailed fingers unexpectedly graceful, he swept into a Scarlatti sonata, followed by a Bach prelude and fugue; once he started playing, he could play for hours.

The first time he had played for Meg, at Ada's urging, the girl had been deeply impressed by his technical skill, but more so by the intelligence and emotive power he brought to his music: a whole new facet to what had seemed a rather sober and unemotional young man. Now she brought out her needlework, threading the needle with strands of scarlet, and began to work, her face dreamy and relaxed in the lamplight. Chris read for a while, then dozed off. Kevin, utterly absorbed, had launched into a series of pieces by Villa-Lobos.

No one heard the tap at the door. It swung open silently and Paul entered. He stood quite still, the music encircling him, his eyes trained on the tableau in front of him: the sleeping child, the musician intent on his gleaming instrument, the girl with the honey-gold hair, her needle splashing crimson on the drift of white fabric in her lap.

He must have made some movement, for the girl suddenly glanced up. She smiled at him, her lips a gentle curve, and beckoned to him. 'Come and join us.'

He moved forward almost reluctantly, bringing a chair into the circle of light and sitting down. Kevin, completely wrapped up in his playing, paid him no attention. Meg smiled again and picked up her needle. 'How's your work going?' she asked softly. He looked at her as if he hardly knew what she meant. 'Is something wrong?' she added quickly.

His face was strained; it needed no great discernment to see the baffled unhappiness in his eyes. Perhaps it was the effect of the music that made him speak without artifice or concealment, his voice pitched low so as not to disturb Kevin. 'When I came in the door, the three of you looked so complete—a unit, like a family. I felt I was an intruder.'

Picking her words with care, she said, 'But that was a false picture. The three of us are not a family, nor will we ever be.'

'I see . . . but to Chris I'm still the intruder.'

In swift compassion she leaned over and rested her hand on his knee, her embroidery forgotten. 'That will mend in time, Paul, I'm sure it will.'

He picked her hand up, absently playing with her slim, ringless fingers. 'He's always been deprived of a proper family. After his mother and I split up, I felt it was best that he stay with her, particularly as she was remarrying immediately. But then when he got ill, she couldn't cope with it—she likes things to go smoothly and without any inconvenience or trouble, does Annette—so now he's in my custody. But nobody could say that he loves me.'

She thought for a minute before speaking. 'Maybe he thinks you took him from his mother. Or maybe he associates you with all the pain and trauma of the hospital and the operation.'

His hand grew still on hers. 'Either or both could be true, Meg. I was told in the hospital simply to wait until Chris puts into his own words what's bothering him . . .'

'But you find the waiting hard.'

He nodded. There seemed nothing more Meg could say, for she knew there was no easy way to solve Chris's self-imposed distancing from his father. She was moved by the intensity of Paul's longing for his son's acceptance, moved, too, that he had so unexpectedly chosen to reveal it to her. Perhaps that was what friends, true friends, were for . . . he was gently stroking her wrist now, his fingers tracing the fragile line of bone and silken skin, his brown eyes looking at but not seeing what he was doing, while all around them the music flung its insistent rhythms.

Deep within her something stirred to life, a yearning and a tenderness that she had never experienced before, in its way as insistent and inevitable as the music. Despite the public notoriety of her past, the parties and escapades, and despite the casual promiscuity of many of her friends,

Meg had always held back from any physical intimacy other than a goodnight kiss or a brief embrace. Even with Philip this had been true. She could not have explained why this had been so. An innate sense of privacy that she did not want violated? A distaste for a series of meaningless love affairs? A physical shrinking from the act itself, an avoidance which more than once had made her wonder if she was normal, or even capable of love? She had never known . . . but now, as this dark-haired stranger stroked her wrist, his mind anywhere but on what he was doing, she felt the first awakening of needs as old as time, and with it a bitter sense of irony that such an intimation of her own sexuality should have come when she was trapped in a wheelchair, an object of pity rather than desire.

With one final singing chord, Kevin's music ended. He put the guitar down, blinking a little as he came back to the present. Without haste Paul put Meg's hand back in her lap and said sincerely, 'You're a fine player, Kevin— I enjoyed that very much. And now I'd better take Chris home and put him to bed.' He got up and went over to the couch, gathering his son into his arms. Chris mumbled something and shoved his head into Paul's sweater, and an expression of such unguarded love passed over Paul's face that Meg felt a lump in her throat. However, as Paul straightened, his eyes leaving his son and going from her to Kevin, the softness vanished, and there was only bleakness and anger, such as she had noticed when he first came in. 'Goodnight,' he said formally. In a moment the door shut behind him.

Kevin yawned widely, apparently blind to any nuances between Paul and Meg. 'How about a coffee before I head out? I'll make it.'

She sat quietly as he moved around the kitchen area, knowing with a fierce certainty that she would have preferred Paul rather than Kevin to have stayed behind. She was crazy even to think such a thing—but crazy or not, it was true.

Kevin came back with the coffee and a plate of cookies, to which he helped himself with absentminded frequency.

'I'm thinking of breaking up with Kathy,' he said. 'Do you know what she's done now?' He launched himself into his latest catalogue of grievances, and Meg listened with only half an ear, nodding at the appropriate intervals, and wishing he would go home. Kevin was a dear, if a long-winded one, but right now she could do without him.

It must have been over an hour before he ran down, his, 'Thanks, Meg, you're a good listener,' making her ashamed of herself.

'I'm sure you'll do whatever is best, Kevin,' she murmured.

'I'm tired of being a doormat,' he said with unusual force. 'It'll do her good to have to come to me for a change. And if she won't—well, I can do without her.' His chin jutted out. 'After all, I could always take you to the craft fair if she won't go.'

Meg smothered a giggle at this most unchivalric offer, and said warmly, 'Don't you drag me into it, Kevin Langley! You've got enough problems with one woman— you don't need two.'

He regarded her soberly. 'There've been times lately I've thought you're three times the woman she'll ever be.'

Before she could realise his intention, he got up, grabbed her by the shoulders, and kissed her hard on the mouth. His beard tickled and his ring was digging into her shoulder blade. When he released her with as little ceremony as he had clutched her, he looked disproportionately pleased with himself. 'I've been wanting to do that for a long time,' he announced.

'Kevin, it's a business partnership we have,' Meg said sharply. 'We also happen to be friends—but that's all.'

'It doesn't have to be.'

'Oh, yes, it does. Apart from anything else, I don't want to be used by you just to make Kathy jealous.'

As soon as she spoke, she regretted her words, for his eyes lit up and it was obvious he had not even thought of that. 'Hey, that's a great idea—you'd better plan on coming to the craft fair with me for sure. That'll show her.'

In terms of the handcrafts he dealt with, Kevin showed a subtlety of judgement that she respected; as a musician she respected him even more. But in his dealings with the opposite sex, he was about as subtle as a ten-ton tank. 'We'll see,' she said forbearingly, instantly reminded of Paul's words earlier in the day—and how long ago that seemed. 'Thank you for coming with the new stuff, Kevin, and thank you for playing—I always enjoy that.'

Fortunately he took the hint. 'Okay. I'll see you soon. Thanks for supper.'

He made no attempt to kiss her again, and as he left, she heaved a sigh of relief. She did hope he wouldn't do anything foolish like become seriously interested in her; she liked the relationship just as it was. After carefully folding up her needlework and putting it away, she got ready for bed, her thoughts swiftly leaving Kevin and going instead to that last image she had of Paul—angry, bitter, somehow threatening. Their brief conversation under cover of the music had been real, she would stake her life on that. Why then had he chosen to withdraw into himself again? It was a mystery, and one she felt helpless to solve.

Wisps of fog, insubstantial as ghosts, still veiled the rocks and inlets of the cove when Meg got up the next morning, and through the mist the cries of the gulls were like the mourning of lost souls. But within an hour the sun had burned through, driving away the sadness and mystery of the fog until it was simply a bright, hot summer day, the first that season. Too warm a day to stay indoors, Meg decided. Letting herself out, she waved to Ben and Chris, who as usual were pottering away behind the woodshed. 'Take me out to Flat Rock, Grandpa?' she called. Leading through the woods along the promontory behind her grandfather's house there was a trail which had been used years ago by the keeper of the lighthouse that perched at the promontory's seaward tip; now overgrown in places, the path was still wide enough for her wheelchair. Flat Rock, named by one of Ada's brood, was about half way out, and overlooked a tiny, crescent-shaped beach of pale sand where generations of island children had learned to swim; it was one of Meg's favourite places.

Ben had ambled over to her, Chris trotting at his side. 'Mind if I leave you there for an hour or so? Promised the young feller I'd run him into Camden this morning to buy a bucket and shovel. Unless you'd like to come with us?'

'No, thanks, Grandpa. I've got a book I want to read. I'd enjoy just sitting in the sun out there.'

He took the handles of her chair and the three of them set off down the trail, Chris chatting away about a fish he had caught off the rocks earlier that morning. In the undergrowth birds rustled and twittered. Tiny twinflowers crowded to the edge of the path, interspersed with clusters of the white-flowered bunchberries. The needles of the hackmatack were a light, fresh green. Meg drew a deep breath of the morning air, clean and sweet and always overlaid with the salt tang of the sea. 'I could manage this path on my own, I should think,' she said, as always disliking the idea of involving other people in her outings, even her grandfather, willing though she knew him to be.

'I wouldn't do that, lass. A few tricky places—especially nearer the rocks.' He was right, she supposed, knowing she should be sensible and accept her limitations; she had plenty of time to learn how, after all.

Bare rock, seamed and eroded, was emerging through the grass and in a few minutes Ben turned to the left where the rock widened out into a flat ledge overlooking the sea. He set the brake on her chair. 'Here we are. Sure you'll be okay on your own, now? Chris and I'll be back for you in a couple of hours.'

'I'll be fine—have fun.' She heard their departing foot-steps across the rock and then she was left alone with only the sounds of the woods and the sea, the murmur of the breeze and the constant ripple of the water. The sun was warm on her back and shoulders. She had put on a halter-top under her shirt, and now she removed the outer gar-ment, closing her eyes and leaning her head back to feel the golden rays on her face, burning orange under her closed lids. The minutes slipped by, without thought, her

whole being absorbed in the sensations of heat and light
and whispering sounds.

It was the raucous, irreverent cawing of a crow that
eventually made her open her eyes. She let out her breath
in a long sigh. In front of her stretched the rocks of the
opposite shore, below and to her right was the rough
pathway that led down to the beach, where the gentle
swell surged and fell in tiny wavelets, crisp as lace. The
water was incredibly blue and very clear; she could see
the serried ridges of sand beneath its surface. Quite
suddenly she was overwhelmed by the longing to be
wading along the shore. To scramble down the path across
the lichened rocks, to feel the shifting grains of sand between her toes, to splash and play in the cold water like a
child. But she couldn't, she couldn't . . . she was chained
to her wheelchair as surely as if links of steel encircled her
ankles. Caught, trapped, held . . . crippled . . .

An ugly sound, compounded of pain and frustration,
burst from her lips. She buried her head in her hands,
tears streaming down her cheeks.

'Meg! What's wrong?'

Like an apparition Paul had appeared in front of her,
half kneeling by her chair so that his face was level with
hers. A sob caught in her throat. In all the long lonely
months since the accident she had never cried in front of
anyone, never allowed another living soul to witness her
attacks of despair and her fears of the future. But now, as
if she was a blind person groping her way, her hands
reached out for him; in her drowned blue eyes was a
wordless plea for comfort.

His arms went around her, gathering her to his chest
and holding her close as her slender frame was torn by
shuddering sobs. 'I can't walk,' she managed to gasp incoherently. 'Oh, Paul, I can't walk!'

She cried until she was exhausted, cried herself into the
emptiness that was not yet peace but rather the absence
of pain. Giving a tremulous sniff, she muttered, 'I need a
handkerchief.'

He pressed a couple of tissues into her hand. 'These'll
have to do—I'm afraid I wasn't prepared.'

She wiped at her wet cheeks and blew her nose, prosaic little actions that were the first return to normality. Avoiding his eyes, she said, 'Thank you—I didn't mean to cry all over you.'

'Tell me about it.'

She gazed out over the blue water, her breath still catching in her throat. 'I wanted to be able to get out of my chair, walk down to the beach and wade in the sea. And I couldn't.'

'I see. Look at me—how long since you've cried like that?'

Reluctantly she met his gaze. 'Oh, ages.'

'Too long, I have no doubt—try not to bottle it up, Meg. It's not good for you.'

Her fingers plucked at her skirt. 'I suppose not.'

He went on steadily, 'I can't make you walk. But I can certainly take you down to the beach—come on.'

Once again she was in his arms, only this time he was carrying her, stepping carefully from rock to rock down the path to the beach. He put her down with her back against a smooth boulder, her face to the sun, and then he took off her shoes so she could feel the heat reflecting from the sand. Still without saying a word, he began unbuttoning his shirt. She waited, too drained of all emotion to be anything but acquiescent to whatever might come next. He shrugged out of his shirt, went to the water's edge and dipped part of it into the water, wringing it out. Then he came back to the girl and very gently wiped the tear-stains from her face.

'I must look awful,' she ventured.

'You look fine to me.'

Ordinary words accompanying a very practical action. Why then was her heart fluttering against her ribs as though a man had never been this close to her before? For he was close, so close that she could see how iris and pupil seemed to merge, dark brown to black; could see the shadows under his collarbones, the sun gleaming on the smooth skin of his shoulders; could feel his breath on her cheek. She could lose herself in the fathomless darkness of those eyes ... lose the Meg that she thought she knew and discover a new woman, a stranger to her, neither Meg nor Margaret, a woman who wanted to reach out and touch the man's sunwarmed shoulders and draw him closer until their lips would meet and the outer world would drop away ...

Her eyes widened in panic and instinctively she shrank back against the rock. He moved back, his face blank of expression, and the moment shattered and was gone. As if nothing had happened—and perhaps for him nothing had, she thought dazedly—he said, 'The water's freezing. I'm not sure you would want to wade.'

'I guess it doesn't warm up enough to swim in until July.'

'Would you like me to get your book?' he asked politely.

She smothered an hysterical urge to giggle. It seemed impossible that five minutes ago she had been in his arms. 'Yes, thank you,' she answered equally politely.

When he came back with it, she said, 'Paul, how did you happen to come here?'

'I met Chris and your grandfather, and they told me where you were. I hadn't explored down here yet, so I decided to kill two birds with one stone.'

'Oh,' she responded uncertainly, not sure she liked his metaphor. Glancing down at her book, she added, 'If I read, what will you do?' She summoned a faint smile. 'Don't go away and leave me here! The tide might come in.'

'I won't go and leave you, Meg.'

There was nothing in his voice to explain why she should feel a frisson along her spine. Hurriedly she opened the book, trying to remember the page where she had finished reading last time. From the corner of her eye she saw Paul lie back on the sand, using his folded-up shirt as a pillow, and close his eyes. Within minutes he was asleep.

She gave up any pretence of reading, letting the book lie open in her lap, instead finding herself studying him intently, as if she could thereby discern why her every encounter with him should affect her so strongly. Long, lean legs in well-fitted jeans. The concavity of his belly and the arch of his rib cage. The tautly muscled chest and arms. And lastly his face. A lock of dark hair had fallen across his forehead. His lashes were absurdly long and thick; Chris's were exactly the same, she remembered. His mouth was relaxed in sleep. A decisive mouth, yet with that contradictory sensual curve to the lower lip. She shivered, wondering what it would be like to be kissed by him.

Her reverie was disturbed by the distant growling of a motor. The sound grew increasingly loud until she could see, coming down the cove, Dave Robert's gold-coloured boat, the *Susan Jane*. Dave was standing by the cockpit in his high boots and dungarees, smoking a pipe, one hand loosely on the wheel; he must have been out to check his lobster pots. She waved at him and he shouted a greeting across the water. From the stern of his boat the wake came out in a vee, washing to the shore after he was out of sight.

Paul flopped over on his stomach with a groan. 'There's no such thing as peace and quiet,' he grumbled.

'Stop complaining,' she began. Then, urgently, 'Paul, what are those scars on your back?' From his ribs to his spine there were two ugly furrows in his flesh.

'Bullet wounds.'

His laconic reply seemed to bring another world into the peaceful little cove. 'Who shot you?' she said faintly.

'A couple of soldiers—I was trying to escape, you see.'

'No, I don't see. Escape from where?'

He rolled over, seeing the genuine horror in her face. 'Don't look so shocked, Meg. I was lucky—I got out of it alive.'

Remembering their conversation at the hotel, she said, 'It must have been when you were overseas, was it? As a journalist?'

'That's right. I've spent a lot of time in Africa over the years, particularly in the newly emerging nations. Unfortunately about a year and a half ago, in search of a story, I got embroiled in a military coup and I didn't get out in time—instead I was thrown in jail, where I stayed for eleven months before there was a change in government and I was released.'

'You still haven't told me who shot you.'

He was trickling sand between his fingers. 'I was trying to escape. It was my own fault, I suppose.'

'Was it that bad?' she asked gently, sure that he was holding something back.

'Bad enough. But it wasn't just that . . .' She waited, holding her breath. 'It all comes back to Chris . . . you see, that was to have been my last trip. I should have been home within the month. Chris's illness hadn't been diagnosed yet—it was a very rare condition—but we knew something was wrong, and Annette was already wanting me to take him. I went overseas to finish up what I was doing, so I could devote all my time to Chris—then all hell broke loose and I ended up in jail. Not knowing when I was going to get out—*if* I was going to get out. Knowing that back home Chris was ill and needed me, but not knowing what was wrong with him . . . God! I thought sometimes I'd go mad shut up in that stinking cell.'

'So that was why you tried to escape . . .'

'Yeah . . . I might as well have saved myself the trouble, because they slapped me in solitary after that.'

'Oh, Paul . . .' Scarcely thinking what she was doing, she reached out her hand and clasped his wrist. 'So when you did finally get back, what happened?'

'Chris's illness had been diagnosed, the surgery was already scheduled and Annette was just about frantic—she'd had all the papers drawn up for a change of custody for over six months.'

To abandon your own child when he was ill and needing you . . . yet to some extent was that not what her own parents had done with her? 'Chris's mother—what's she like?'

He gazed across the quiet blue waters of the cove. 'Very rich. Very beautiful. Very spoiled. I think the reason I fell for her so heavily in the first place was that she was the first woman I'd ever met who wasn't after my money— my father left me money, you see; he made a mint out of various forms of land speculation, legal and quasi-legal. It wasn't until after I married her that I discovered she was totally incapable of functioning on her own. What I'd thought of as the rather charming way she clung to me turned out to be a total dependence on whomever was nearest. On my first trip overseas after our marriage when I wasn't available, she found someone else. After that, I tried to stay home and spend more time with her. But I couldn't give up my work, it was too important to me— and she couldn't give up the other men. So we separated. As soon as the legalities were dealt with, she married Oliver, who dotes on her and hovers around her twenty-four hours a day—they're much better suited than she and I ever were.'

'Do you still love her?'

'Heavens, no. I'm not sure now that I ever did.'

'Does Chris?'

'You tell me,' he said heavily. 'Any time I've tried to find out, he's clammed right up.' He shot her a wry glance, and used the identical words that Kevin had used the night before. 'You must be a good listener, Meg—I don't normally talk about myself this much.' It seemed perfectly natural that he should move nearer to her, lean forward, and kiss her very gently on the mouth.

For Meg time stopped. The image of his face, so close to hers, burned itself in her brain just as his lips burned against her mouth. Shaken, she knew that for him it was merely a gesture of gratitude for her attention and understanding; she was too frightened to examine what it had been for her.

She must have recoiled, for he said roughly. 'Don't look like that. I'm not about to seduce you.'

'I—I know you're not. It wasn't . . .' Her voice trailed off.

'I'm not Kevin—is that what's wrong?'

Completely bewildered, she repeated stupidly, 'Kevin?'

'Don't pretend you don't know what I'm talking about.'

'I'm sorry, but I don't.'

'Come off it. I'm sure Kevin did more than kiss you

after I left the two of you alone together last night.'

Belatedly she found her tongue, and with it lost her temper. 'Oh? And just what do you think Kevin and I were doing?'

'Do I have to spell it out for you?'

'Obviously you do!'

'You went to bed together, didn't you?'

'No, as a matter of fact, we didn't,' she raged. 'Do you want to know what we did? We discussed Kevin's girl-friend. At considerable length, I might add.'

'You mean he never even kissed you?'

A denial on the tip of her tongue, she suddenly blushed scarlet, remembering that he *had* kissed her. 'He did, yes,' she admitted. 'But he only wants to make Kathy jealous.'

'Who are you kidding, Meg—she wasn't even there!'

'Neither were you—so why are *you* jealous?' she demanded recklessly. 'What's it to you whether I kiss Kevin or not?'

He drew back, and she knew she had struck home. Very quietly he said, 'I wish I had the answer to that question, but I don't. So maybe we'd better drop the sub-ject.' He surveyed her temper-flushed cheeks and brilliant sea-blue eyes and added, equally softly, 'Although maybe I'm a fool to do so . . . I wonder if you have any idea how beautiful you look, Meg.'

The pink in her cheeks was from more than temper now, and she lowered her eyes, unable to meet his level gaze. She had been called beautiful many times by many different men back in Vancouver, and had always shrugged it off, even to the point of wondering cynically if they would find her as beautiful were she not rich. But Paul Moreton, on his own admission, had plenty of money of his own, and he was seeing a very different woman from the old Margaret with her upswept hairdo and daring make-up, her dashing, original clothes always chosen with a view to shock and surprise. She was Meg now, with her hair blowing free in the salt breeze and her face innocent of adornment, and Paul's quietly spoken praise of her beauty affected her more than she cared to admit.

'Look at me, Meg.'

Unwillingly she raised her eyes; she was becoming frightened again, knowing in her heart that he was a very different man from any she had ever known back in Vancouver. Already she sensed in him hidden depths; there was will power in the strongly carved lines of his face, a hint of sensuality in the well-shaped mouth. It would be dangerous to become involved with him at anything other than a superficial level; yet because he was the man he was, all her involvement with him had been anything but superficial.

His next words could only bear out what she had been thinking. 'I want to kiss you again,' he said.

'No, Paul.' She pressed back against the rock, her voice oddly breathless.

'Why not?'

Because I'm afraid of you, she could have said—afraid of what you might do to me. 'Maybe I don't want to,' she hazarded.

'I don't believe you. You want to, all right. But you're scared to.'

'All right, then, so I'm scared,' she said roundly. 'I've made a new life for myself here, Paul, and it hasn't been easy—so I guess I don't want someone like you breezing in and turning it upside down.'

'So you do admit I could do that?'

She frowned, irritated with herself for revealing so much. 'I was speaking generally.'

'I think you were being very specific. But what you're really saying, Meg, is that you're determined to hide yourself away from life—you're not going to take the risk of any kind of involvement.'

He was entirely too discerning. 'I have a perfect right to decide what I want to do with my life,' she snapped.

'I don't think anyone has the right to turn his or her back on the world.'

'It's fine for you to be so philosophical—but you're forgetting that I'm tied to a wheelchair. I'm not a normal woman, Paul Moreton, so stop talking as if I am.'

'I loathe that word normal,' he retorted. 'It must be

one of the most meaningless words in the dictionary. You're a beautiful young woman who's capable of leading a much fuller and richer life than you're leading now—it only took me a couple of days to see that.'

'And to decide it was your mission in life to put things to right?' she asked waspishly.

'Don't be bitchy, Meg. We decided we were friends, remember? As your friend, I want more for you than you're apparently willing to settle for.'

Irrelevantly she noticed how the breeze was disordering the silky thickness of his hair. He was still far too close for comfort, so she shifted her position slightly on the yielding sand. His eyebrow quirked as if he knew exactly what she had been thinking. 'It's time I was getting back,' she said idiotically.

'All the more reason for a kiss before we go,' was the lazy response.

'Paul, please——'

He rested his hands on her shoulders; they were surprisingly heavy. 'Relax, Meg,' he drawled. 'This isn't going to hurt a bit. In fact, you might find you even enjoy it.'

While he was speaking, he had been bringing his face closer to hers. Instinctively she closed her eyes as his lips brushed her forehead and drifted across her cheekbone to eventually come to rest on her mouth. She held herself rigidly, fighting against any response, helplessly aware of how much in his power she was; almost her last coherent thought was that she certainly couldn't run away . . . His hands had moved lingeringly up her neck to cup her face and he was nibbling gently at her lips. Then there was the warmth of his mouth full on hers and everything was blotted out but the sheer sensual delight of a kiss that seemed to go on forever. The warmth spread from her mouth through her whole body, flooding her with an incredible sweetness that brought in its wake an aching for something more: pleasure and pain mingled in a way she had never experienced before. She was scarcely aware that her hands had slid up his chest to clasp him by the shoulders; she no longer felt the dig of the rock in her back or the heat of the sand on her bare legs.

Paul must have felt her complete surrender, for there could be no mistaking the melting of her body against his. Only then did he very slowly release her.

She opened her eyes, the pulse in her throat throbbing against the skin. He was watching her closely and it took a moment for his complete lack of expression to penetrate her brain. She moved back slightly, feeling the first quiver of unease. With an almost clinical detachment in his voice he said, 'If I didn't know better, Margaret Cairns, I'd say you'd never been kissed before.'

It was like a dash of cold water in her face. 'What do you mean?' she stammered. 'Of course I have been!'

'Perhaps I phrased that wrongly. You've been kissed before—that implies a certain passivity on your part. But have you ever responded like that before?'

She had not, of course. She stared at him dumbly, hating his perspicacity, and even beginning to wonder if the kiss had been merely an experiment for him, a cold-blooded attempt to assess her experience—or rather, lack of it.

'You needn't bother to answer, because I know the answer already,' he said softly. 'Gossip columns notwithstanding, you're as innocent as a newborn babe, Meg. And wheelchair notwithstanding, you have all of a woman's passion and needs.'

In a few short moments she had plummeted from the magic of his kiss to the chilling realisation that that kiss had meant nothing to him. He had the power to play with her emotions, and were he to kiss her again, she doubted she would have the strength of will to resist him. What strange twist of chemistry gave him that power, she did not know; all she knew was that she feared it. She had said a while ago he could turn her world upside down, and now in truth he had done so, revealing to her a woman she had not even known existed. 'I want to go home,' she said, her voice shaking a little despite herself.

'Very well—I'll take you back.' He squatted on his heels beside her. 'But I want you to remember what happened here this morning.'

As if she could ever forget . . . 'Under the circumstances, what happened here this morning should never have happened,' she said coldly. 'Please take me home.'

He picked her up and she stared straight ahead of her, bracing herself against any appreciation of the strength of his arms, or the clean, masculine scent of his skin. It was a relief to be back in her chair, with Paul behind her; more of a relief that their journey back to the fish shack was accomplished in total silence. But as he left her at the door, he said casually, 'Ben mentioned going out in the boat this afternoon, he wants to set a few more traps. I'll come and get you whenever he's ready.'

'No, thank you,' she said with somewhat overdone politeness.

'Don't give me a hard time, Meg.'

Ignoring the glint of humour in those dark eyes, she said frostily, 'I would prefer not to go.'

'I daresay.' He raised one hand in a mocking salute. 'It'll probably be around two.' Then he was walking away from her, across the grass to Ada's.

Meg let herself into the shack, banging the door behind her as loudly as she could. The room that had become home in the past three months looked exactly as it had earlier that morning; it was she who had changed.

She had sometimes wondered about herself during the latter years in Vancouver. The men she had associated with had many of them been good-looking, comfortably off, well-educated, good company. But they had all left her totally unmoved. She had been wined and dined, she had danced and skiied, she had flirted and teased—but sooner or later with each one she had lightly kissed them on the cheek and said goodbye, without a moment's regret. She had wondered if something was wrong with her, if there was a basic flaw in her character or upbring-ing that made her incapable of any deeper attachment— of loving a man. The word 'frigid' had even occasionally surfaced in her brain, for she had never had any desire for one of the casual affairs so prominent among her crowd. Even Philip, to whom she had been closer than anyone, had never tempted her to that.

Today Paul Moreton had revealed to her that she was indeed truly a woman. But now it was too late . . . her head bowed, her hands clutching the arms of her chair, she fought back the misery that clogged her throat, and even more vainly, fought back the formulation of a thought that could bring nothing but useless regret: if only she had met Paul Moreton a year ago, when she was whole and free. If only, if only . . .

CHAPTER FOUR

WHEN the knock came at the door that afternoon, Meg was sitting by the window working at her embroidery, her needle flashing in the light. But when she called, 'Who is it?' the person who entered was not Paul, but Ben.

'Ready, lass? I was downright pleased when Paul told me you were coming. I've been wanting to get you out in the boat ever since you came here.' Dubiously he eyed her short-sleeved top. 'Better take a sweater, though, it will be cooler on the water. Chris is glad you're coming, too.'

She had opened her mouth to protest, to say she wasn't going, but her grandfather's pleasure was so genuine, so guileless, that she could not do it. And Paul, she would be willing to bet, had known this would happen; that was why he had sent Ben, rather than coming to get her himself. 'I'll get a sweater,' she said in a resigned voice.

Chris and Paul were waiting down at the wharf. Chris came running to meet her. 'Hi, Meg! Ben's got the traps on the boat already. We're going to piggyback you down the ladder. I hope you won't get seasick—do you think you will?'

Interpreting this to mean that Chris was probably afraid of getting seasick himself, she said diplomatically, 'I think it's too calm today, Chris. Did you have fun this morning?'

Chatting away, Chris accompanied her to the wharf, where Paul said urbanely, 'Glad you decided to come, Meg.'

She glared at him, saying sweetly, 'You may not be quite so glad by the time you've got me down that ladder.'

'No problem—you'll see.'

Nor was it. In no time she was seated on the deck in

her chair, which had been wedged between two heavy
packing cases, and an old blanket had been tucked around
her legs. Paul was up by the wheel, talking to Ben. Chris
perched on the box beside her, his eyes brimming with
excitement as Ben started the motor and eased away from
the wharf, making a semi-circle across the cove and heading towards the inlet. As if by a signal the herring gulls
rose from the rocks and swooped in their wake. Along the
shore the ochre-coloured seaweed swayed lazily in the
tide; the sun glittered on the water, so bright that it hurt
the eyes. They passed the beach on their right, then a few
minutes later the white-painted lighthouse that was
perched on the outermost tip of the island.

Harriet III chugged out into the open sea, her prow
lifting to meet the swell. The wind had freshened; the
horizon was a knife-sharp edge, pale blue to deep blue.
They followed the shoreline for about fifteen minutes until
they came to the loosely strung out line of black and white
buoys that marked the locations of the lobster traps. 'They
belong to one of Ada's sons,' Meg explained to Chris.
'Ben just helps out. They lost a few traps in the last storm,
so these new ones are replacements.'

Ben pulled back on the throttle and *Harriet III* slowly
lost momentum, drifting with the tide. From a strong-
smelling barrel by the cabin Ben extracted a couple of
mackerel, cutting them into fair-sized chunks. Opening
the slats on the nearest trap, he shoved a couple of pieces
of fish on the nail sticking up from the floor of the trap:
the lobster would crawl into the trap to get the bait, and
be unable to leave through the chamber's funnel-shaped
opening.

Paul hoisted the trap over to the side of the boat and
dropped it into the sea, the yellow nylon twine snaking
behind it until last of all the buoy splashed into the water.
They proceeded a little farther down the coast and the
operation was repeated. Chris by now had clambered into
Meg's lap and was leaning against her, his dark hair
tickling her chin as he watched the pile of heaped-up traps
diminish one by one. The girl sat very still, with every
fibre of her being aware of the child's weight, of his bony

shoulder digging into her breast, sensations that para-
doxically aroused in her both a sense of fulfilment, of being
needed, yet equally a bittersweet longing for a child she
could call her own. That would never happen now, she
knew, and briefly she allowed herself the luxury of leaning
her cheek against the silken head, her eyes shut, her whole
being focussed on the small boy she held; because her eyes
were shut, she did not see Paul watching them, his dark
eyes very intent, his expression unreadable. What did
bring her back to earth was Chris himself. Wriggling to
get free, he said, 'I want to put the fish on the nail—will
Ben let me?'

Her even voice giving no indication of the turmoil of
emotion within, she said, 'Why don't you ask him? The
only thing you have to watch out for is the rope when the
trap goes overboard.'

Clutching the boxes for support, Chris made his way
forward. Meg watched him go, wondering at the elusive
bond that Chris seemed to feel towards her. It had only
taken him a few short days to reach the level of trust and
liking when he would jump into her lap; yet she knew
intuitively he would not do that with his father, and
wished, not for the first time, that there was something
she could do to help that relationship.

By now they were well along the coastline, and there
was only one trap left. Idly she watched the trio up by
the cockpit, hearing the mingling of the three voices,
treble, tenor and bass, seeing the flurry of activity as the
last trap was dropped into the sea. Then Ben flung some
usless scraps of bait overboard and the air was suddenly
full of screaming, diving gulls, so close that she could see
their predatory hooked beaks and the droplets of water
on their sleek white plumage. They were wheeling and
swooping against the sun, their wingtips touched with
gold, and suddenly for Meg everything coalesced into one
of those moments of perfect unity: the slap of waves against
the prow, the rocking of the boat, the salt breeze tangling
her hair, the golden birds against a golden sun ... she
threw back her head to feel the heat on her face, filled
with a sense of freedom and an inexpressible joy.

A hand came to rest lightly on her shoulder. It was Paul, and she was glad that it was he. Before she could think better of it, she said spontaneously, 'I'm so glad I came! And it was really because of you that I did.' She gave him the full benefit of her generous smile, something of the joy she had felt still lingering in her face.

'A pleasure.' He sat down on one of the boxes, his back to the cabin. Ben had swung *Harriet III* round for the return trip, one hand on the throttle, the other on Chris's shoulder as he let the little boy hold the wheel. At full throttle the engine drowned out the sound of any voices so that Meg and Paul could have been alone. Bringing his head close to hers, the wind whipping his hair, Paul said seriously, 'Meg, I'd like the three of us to spend more time together.' He raised his hand. 'Just hear me out before you say anything. I'm beginning to think fate must have been on my side that night I came to the island—I can't imagine that I could have found a place, or people, better suited to Chris. Ben, Ada, and you ... Chris took to you from the start, you know that as well as I do. I think it would be good for him if the three of us could be together every afternoon, for instance. I have to work on the book in the morning, and you have your commitments to Kevin—but we could take the afternoons off, couldn't we?'

'I suppose so,' she said uncertainly.

'I want the best for my son, Meg, and right now I think he needs the kind of companionship you can provide.'

With the memory of Chris's bony little body curled in her arms, it was hard to resist Paul's plea. But the other thing she could not forget was the kiss on the beach, and the devastating effect it had had on her. Paul was presenting his proposal as if it revolved totally around Chris; what it would also mean was that she and Paul would spend more time together—and what would that entail?

Her indecision must have shown on her face. He said bluntly, 'I'm not asking for any heavy emotional involvement, and there'll be no repeat of what happened this morning. I'm just asking you to help Chris.'

He made it sound so simple—so simple that she did not see how she could refuse. And why should she? she thought rebelliously. Against her better judgment she had allowed herself to be coerced into this boat trip, and the result had been pure pleasure; she had felt fully alive, at one with her surroundings in a way she had not been since the days when she would gallop across a windswept field or ski down a mountain slope. Perhaps Paul was right and she had been hiding herself away, settling for less than she had to ... It had only taken a second or two for these thoughts to cross her mind, yet despite them, she was still reluctant to fully commit herself. 'We could try,' she said hesitantly. 'If we found it wasn't working out, we could always drop the idea.'

'It will work out,' Paul said confidently. 'Tomorrow let's take the car and go farther down the shore. Who knows, we might even find Bayfield!'

She laughed, feeling a rush of anticipation for the next day. It would be fun to explore the coastline, she thought, ignoring the fact that any of the anticipation could be related to spending more time with the dark-haired man at her side.

When they docked at the wharf, Ada came down to invite them all for dinner. Her kitchen was filled with the smell of roasting turkey and the fragrance of apple pie and fresh rolls. 'Now you take off those boots, Ben Cairns,' she ordered as they arrived. 'And hang up your oilskins in the back porch.'

Meekly Ben did as he was told. It hadn't taken Meg long to recognise Ada's passion for cleanliness, and she could still remember Ben's remark when he had first brought her here that Ada's curtains were so highly starched you could cut yourself on the edges. The old cliché of being able to eat off the kitchen floor would certainly apply at Ada's, she thought now, eyeing the gleaming tiles reflectively; her own mother shared this same need for order and cleanliness, yet with a vital difference: Sandra Cairns disliked people disordering her elegant and tastefully decorated house, whereas Ada's door was always open for family and friends.

Ben carved the turkey and then they all sat around the kitchen table, the westering sun slanting through the crisp gingham curtains. Finally Ben leaned back, replete. 'That was quite a spread, Ada.' He watched as she poured him a second cup of tea, adding just the amount of milk that he liked. 'It's like I keep telling you—you'd make me a fine wife.'

'Come on, now, Ben Cairns, we've all heard that before!'

'I figure I might as well keep trying,' Ben remarked. 'One of these days you might say yes just to shut me up.'

'I doubt that, now,' she said briskly, pouring Chris another glass of milk. 'You and I are quite comfortable as we are, living next door to each other—why should we change anything?'

'Because I love your apple pie?' Ben said hopefully.

'Go on with you! You know you're over here just as soon as I take anything out of the oven as it is. More tea, Paul?' For Ada the discussion was clearly closed, and Ben subsided, philosophically drinking his tea and accepting another piece of pie. Meg smiled at him, knowing it probably wouldn't be long before he asked Ada the same question again, undoubtedly to receive the same answer. Not for the first time, she wondered at Ada's adamant refusal to marry Ben; she was fond of him, there was no question of that, and either one of them would be lost without the other's company. It was strange . . .

After the meal was cleared away and the dishes washed and dried, they played a few simple card games for Chris's benefit. Once he was in bed a cut-throat game of hearts ensued, during which Paul showed a new side of his character: a sense of fun, of pure devilment that had them all in stitches. Finally Ben pulled his old-fashioned gold watch from his pocket; it was attached to his waistband by a narrow chain. 'If I'm going out with your son Randall tomorrow morning to check those traps, Ada, I'd better get to bed,' he said. And to Paul, 'You were lucky with the cards, only reason you won.'

'I must get home, too,' said Meg. 'Thank you, Ada. 'Night, Ben, Paul.'

'I'll see you tomorrow after lunch—rain or shine,' Paul promised.

She was assailed by a sudden wave of doubt, but had no chance to express it, for Ben was saying, 'Come on, Meg, I'll see you down to the shack.'

Outside the air was cool, the black sky sprinkled with glimmering stars. The water of the cove murmured and sighed. In silence the old man and the young girl went across the grass towards the grey outline of the shack. At the door Meg looked up at her grandfather, his jacket a paler outline against the sky. Something in the stoop of his shoulders made her say impulsively, 'Surely she'll marry you one day, Grandpa.'

'Maybe . . . maybe not. Trouble is, I think she's still in love with Jonathan, for all that he's been dead these ten years. He was a fine man and my best friend—I can hardly blame her, I suppose.'

'What happened to him?' she asked softly.

'Drowned offshore in a spring storm—him and one of his sons. Don't think Ada ever got over it.' He sighed. 'Makes it hard sometimes.'

'She really cares for you, I'm sure.'

'Guess so.'

'Of course she does, Grandpa.' She brought his gnarled old hand up to her cheek. 'Just keep trying, okay?'

'Not got much choice,' was the phlegmatic reply. Awkwardly he patted her shoulder. 'Glad you're here, Meg. Apart from your father, who hasn't been back here in thirty years, you're all the family I've got.'

'He never liked it here, did he?' she ventured; the subject of her father had not come up before.

'Couldn't wait to shake the sand out of his boots—he was like his mother in that respect. But that's enough of that—see you tomorrow.'

She watched his figure disappear into the darkness and in a moment or two the kitchen light came on in his house. He hadn't had a happy life, she was sure, for it was obvious that his son's defection from the only world Ben loved and knew had hurt him badly; and now he was intimating that his wife Harriet had never liked it either.

At least she, Meg, was here, she thought fiercely. And she
loved Cairns Island . . . had loved it from the first moment
she saw it. The grey rocks and the pounding surf were in
her blood, home to her in a way the manicured lawns
and elegant mansion in Vancouver had never been. She
belonged here, and here she would stay . . .

Her brow puckered thoughtfully. Perhaps that was why
she reacted so strongly to Paul's presence—he was dis-
turbing a world whose peace and beauty she cherished. A
vagrant breeze blew across her bare arms, and she
shivered. It was time for bed . . .

When Meg looked back on the days that followed, they
seemed bathed in perpetual sunshine. It must have rained
sometimes. There must have been fog and wind and
drizzle. But it was the sunshine she remembered. Day after
day of golden sunshine.

The three of them, she, Paul, and Chris, roamed the
countryside, following at their whim the maze of side
roads that led to tiny fishing coves and often deserted
beaches. They constructed exotic sandcastles with Chris;
they ate lobster fresh out of the pot with their fingers;
they picked wild strawberries and made daisy chains. In
the coastal towns they visited art galleries, craft shops,
and museums; in the waterfront city of Halifax they ate
Greek and Italian and Chinese food and went to movies
and mingled with the crowds of residents and tourists on
the busy sidewalks. As the days passed Meg lost her caution and uncertainty; her fear of Paul Moreton receded to
the very back of her mind, forgotten and ignored. He was
the perfect companion, intelligent and witty, sensitive, yet
full of fun. At first, out of months-long habits, she resisted
a lot of his plans. Of course she couldn't do that . . . she'd
never manage to do this . . . but, inexorably, he insisted;
and as he did so, her horizons widened and she gradually
lost the crippling selfconsciousness that had so hampered
her in the past.

As she had forgotten her fear of him, so she had thrust
into her subconscious the memory of that devastating kiss.
Although of necessity he had to touch her, picking her up

and carrying her to places where her wheelchair would not go, he never prolonged his hold and his hands were as impersonal as those of a brother. Other than that he never touched her; he never kissed her or in any way indicated to her that she was an attractive and desirable woman. And because she was discovering so much about herself, and enjoying herself in a way she never had before, she was content to have it so.

Besides Paul, there was Chris . . . as the days drifted by, it did seem as though Chris was edging closer to his father. It was still noticeable that he never called him 'Dad', but at least he would voluntarily tuck his hand in Paul's as they walked along the cliffs, or would accept a piggyback ride if Paul waded into the sea, digging his heels into his father's ribs and shrieking with excitement if he was splashed by the breakers. He was a far cry from the thin, pale little boy who had arrived in the storm. Ada's cooking had done wonders for his weight, while the hours he spent outdoors had tanned his skin and dusted his nose with freckles.

Caught up as she was in the present with all its activities and fun, Meg did not stop to assess her relationships with Chris, either. She loved it when he hurtled into her lap. She was touched when he saved up his money and bought her a gaudy necklace of coloured glass, and she wore it often. But she never looked ahead into the future, into the autumn days when he would undoubtedly be gone. The present was enough for her, and she threw herself into it wholeheartedly, blind that it might present dangers . . .

Then, one afternoon in July, everything changed. Chris had stayed home that day, because Ben and Randall MacKinnon had promised to take him jigging mackerel. Because their afternoons together had become such a habit, Meg raised no demur when Paul suggested they drive to South Point; lately she had been studying the local wildflowers to make her own designs for crewel embroidery, and the meadows at the Point would furnish her with some different specimens. When they got there, Paul parked by the side of the road and carried her up the hillside to the edge of the field where a row of maples

cast shadows on the grass. She gazed around her with
pleasure, unconscious of the fact that as she did so, Paul
was studying her. To her right a thrush warbled among
the shadowed trees; to her left was the open expanse of
the meadow. A carpet of delicate bluets nestled in the
grass where she was sitting, while ragged-robin, but-
tercups, and black-eyed Susans raised their bright faces to
the sun in a profusion of fragile beauty that delighted her.
On the other side of the road was the unimaginatively
named South Inlet, its surface smooth as glass; in the
shallows a heron stood statue-still on its long, thin legs, its
beak poised to catch an unwary frog or fish. It was low
tide and to her nostrils drifted the pungent odour of
seaweed exposed to the heat, overpowering the more
subtle fragrance of flowers and grass.

'What a beautiful place,' she said softly, almost reluctant to disturb the somnolent afternoon by the sound of
her own voice.

'It is, isn't it?' said Paul, his gaze still fastened on her
upturned profile.

They were rarely alone together, for if Chris wasn't
with them, which was unusual, Ben or Ada was. But now
seemed to Meg the perfect opportunity to say something
she had been wanting to express to Paul for some time.
She lay back in the grass with unselfconscious grace,
her hands linked behind her head, quite heedless of how
this drew the thin material of her shirt taut across her
breasts. Her eyes reflecting the clear blue of the sky above,
she said dreamily, 'I'm so glad you came to the island,
Paul.'

'Oh . . . why?'

Nothing in his voice to alert her to what was to come.
She picked a stem of grass and chewed on it abstractedly,
thinking of what she wanted to say. 'After the accident
when I went back to my father's house in Vancouver . . .'
For a moment she glanced up at him, admiring the way
his strong, angular profile was silhouetted against the sky.
'Isn't that interesting, I don't think of it as home any
more. Anyway, when I got out of the hospital and went
back there, I really thought my life was over. It would

just be a question from then on of getting through the days—they would all be alike, you see. Nothing to distinguish one from another. And it was like that . . . dreadful.' Her face clouded briefly. 'But then the invitation came from my grandfather, whom I'd never met, to spend the summer on his island here on the east coast. I had nothing to lose. So, totally against my father's wishes, I came. I've already told you how Ben had the old shack fixed up for me so I could be independent, and how I started working for Kevin and earning money of my own. And then you and Chris came and things changed again. Do you know what you've done for me?'

'Why don't you tell me?'

'You've brought me to life again. Look at all the things we've done in the past couple of weeks—things I never thought I'd ever be able to do again. And look at the fun we've had! I don't think I've ever laughed so much or enjoyed myself as much in my life before. But it's even more than that. Because of all the different places we've been—restaurants and theatres and shops—I seem to have lost a lot of the selfconsciousness I used to have about being in a wheelchair. And it's largely thanks to you.' She smiled up at him, the sun full in her eyes so that she could not see his expression. 'Right now, I feel as though I could go anywhere, do anything.'

Very quietly he said, 'Good . . . I've been waiting to hear you say something to that effect.'

'Oh? You mean you saw what was happening to me?'

'Oh, yes. I wanted it to happen.'

Meg frowned slightly, wishing she could see his face, for there was a note in his voice she did not quite understand. 'You mean, you did it on purpose?'

'More or less. I wanted you to move out of that narrow little world on the island. To realise how much you were capable of doing.'

'Then you've succeeded.'

'In that much, yes.'

Again she felt faintly uneasy. Nevertheless, she decided to finish what she wanted to say. 'You know, even after you and Chris are gone, I'll still feel so much freer than before you came. I do appreciate what you've done for me, Paul.'

'I've never said anything about leaving.'

'Well, no—but I'm sure you won't stay on Cairns Island all winter.'

'I have to take Chris up to Toronto in a few days for a check-up with the heart specialist. While I'm there, I'm going to put my house on the market. Then when I come back I'm going to start looking for a place in this area. I already have a couple of leads.'

She had been living totally in the present ever since Paul had arrived, and one of the reasons for that had been her assumption that both Paul and Chris would only be temporary people in her life, summer visitors who would leave when the autumn came. That they might remain in the area had never occurred to her, and she felt her heart lift at the prospect. She had consciously been endeavouring not to get too attached to Chris, knowing he would be leaving in a couple of months; now that there was the chance she would still be able to see him all next winter, she could acknowledge how fond of him she was . . .

'You're not saying much.'

She looked up at him. 'You took my by surprise. I had no idea you were thinking of settling around here.'

'Do you have any idea why I want to do it?'

She searched his face for clues, finding none. 'It's certainly a fine place for Chris. He looks so much better than he did when he came.'

'That's right. And some of that's the place and some of that's you. I want you to marry me, Meg.'

She stared at him, her jaw dropping, wondering if she had heard rightly. '*What* did you say?'

'I want you to marry me, Meg.'

She propped herself up on one elbow. 'If this is your idea of a joke, I don't think much of it!'

'I'm not joking—I've never been more serious in my life.'

'Then you're crazy!'

'That's not very flattering to either one of us.'

'Oh, do stop!' she cried. 'If you *are* asking me to marry you, then the answer's no.' Her lips compressed, she glared down at the still waters of the inlet, knowing the day's beauty was ruined for her. 'Let's go home.'

'Not yet. Not until we've finished discussing this.'

'There's nothing more to say.'

'Of course there is.' He took her by the arm. 'Just get over the idea that I'm doing this for some kind of a joke—I'm not. I want to marry you, and I want more of an answer from you than I've got so far. You can't just brush this off as if it hadn't happened.'

Meg pushed her hair back from her eyes, a slight tremor in her fingers. There had been anger in his voice, and conviction, and something else—hurt? She said slowly. 'All right, I hear what you're saying, and I apologise. But that doesn't alter my decision. You know as well as I do that I can never marry you, Paul.'

'If I thought that, I wouldn't have asked you.'

His obduracy was like the hard, unyielding face of a cliff; like the waves of the sea, she could dash herself against it and only fall back in defeat. 'Why *did* you ask me?'

'Because Chris needs a mother. Because I like you and respect you.'

There could be no doubting his honesty. She said drily, 'The usual reason people get married is because they love each other.'

Just as drily he replied, 'I thought I loved Annette, but I can't imagine a greater disaster than that marriage. The past couple of weeks have shown me that we enjoy each other's company, we like doing the same things, we get along well together. You're very intelligent. I like your sense of humour. And right from the start I knew you were beautiful.'

'What a cold-blooded assessment of all my virtues!' She added shrewishly, 'I also have a temper—you forgot that.'

Incredibly Paul laughed. 'I already told you that I like a woman to stand up for herself.' Sobering almost immediately, he went on, 'Maybe the love would come in time, Meg. I don't know. But I figured it was better to be honest. After all, you're not in love with me, are you?'

'Of course not,' she said shortly.

'But you're fond of Chris.'

Baffled, she stared up at him, knowing they were back where they had started. 'Yes, I am. But I can't marry you because of that.' She paused, knowing that somehow she had to convince him of the genuineness of her refusal. 'Now let *me* be honest with you, Paul. I won't marry you or anyone else as long as I'm in a wheelchair. I couldn't be a proper mother to Chris nor a proper wife to you. I certainly wouldn't be able to have children of my own. Don't you see? It's impossible!'

'Yet five minutes ago you were telling me how free and independent you'd felt since you met me.'

'That's different! That's outings to the beach, and going to the movies and trips to town – that's not marriage.' She had picked a daisy and was shredding off the petals one by one, her movements jerky and unco-ordinated.

'Let's try this, then.'

She glanced up, the flowerhead clutched in her fingers. He had turned to face her, his long legs stretched out on the grass beside her, and she read the purpose in his face. 'Don't, Paul——'

She might just as well not have spoken. His mouth seized hers and then he was on top of her, his weight crushing her into the grass. She beat at his shoulders with her fists, trying to jerk her head free. His hands caught at her wrists, holding them captive, and the touch of his mouth gentled.

Meg ceased struggling and lay very still, her eyes closed as her senses were assailed by feelings too strong to be ignored or fought against. The heat of his body through his thin shirt. The bite of his fingers around her wrists. The questing, almost tender movements of his lips against hers, as if he was seeking a reaction from her, even begging for it. Tentatively she began kissing him back.

It was as if he caught fire from her shy, innocent response, for his kiss grew deeper, more demanding. He released her wrists and his hands moved down the length of her body. He had picked her up and carried her many times in the past few weeks, so in that sense she was familiar with his touch. But this was different. It was as if he was trying to learn every line of her frame through his hands, and commit it to memory. He smoothed the slope of her shoulders and followed the long curve of her spine to her hips. He caressed the nape of her neck, his fingers tangled in her thick hair. Her lips parted involuntarily and his mouth probed hers, filling her with an ache of desire that obliterated any remnant of caution or reason. She ran her fingers through the silky hair around his ears and her mouth grew bolder, opening to him, saying more clearly than words that she wanted what he was giving.

He rolled sideways so that they were facing each other, and then, like a stroking of fire, she felt his hands move from her waist up to her breasts, moulding their fullness, teasing and tantalising the tips to hardness. Deep in her throat she moaned with pleasure. Paul began to unfasten the buttons of her shirt one by one and then he undid the front clasp of her bra, pushing back the fabric to expose her milk-white skin to the sun, and to the touch of his fingers.

When his mouth left hers, she opened blurred blue eyes to find his face only inches away, his eyes burning like coals, his breathing rapid, while all the time his hands continued their leisurely, intimate exploration. Of its own accord her body arched towards him, and he flung his thigh across her legs, drawing them closer. His lips wandered down the slender line of her throat, nibbling at the sweet-scented skin, until they found the swelling, blue-veined breast.

Time stopped, for there was nothing in the world but the exquisite torment of his lovemaking. Her head was thrown back, her nails digging into the taut muscles of his back, holding him close, where he belonged, she thought dazedly. Where no one else but he had ever been . . .

'You want me, don't you, Meg?' His voice was rough with passion.

The pliant, yielding lines of her body must have been answer enough. 'Oh, yes,' she whispered.

'We could make love here in the grass . . . you'd like that, wouldn't you?'

She nodded, murmuring, 'I never knew it could be like this.'

'I want you to marry me, Meg.'

Her eyes flew open as she tensed in his hold. It was the third time he had said it, and this time the words struck a chord of pure agony that in a split second dissipated the wonder of her body's awakening. She was suddenly conscious of a rock digging into her spine, of an insect crawling on her arm; and worse, of her naked breasts. She grabbed her shirt and pulled the edges together to cover herself, her cheeks scarlet. 'I'm not going to,' she said raggedly, her eyes appalled. 'Did you think you could make me change my mind? Is that why you kissed me?'

'I kissed you because I wanted to. But what just happened between us makes nonsense of your statement that you wouldn't be a proper wife to me.' He grinned at her so unexpectedly and so infectiously that she almost smiled back. 'The odds are you'd make me a delightfully improper wife!'

Irritated with herself for so nearly being beguiled into laughter, Meg said sharply, 'I'm not going to make you any kind of a wife, and that's that!'

He sat up, pulling her up to face him, his grip like steel traps. 'Listen to me, Meg. For some reason, and don't let's analyse it even if we could, we click, you and I, as far as sex is concerned. The chemistry's right. I have a feeling that happens more rarely than one might suppose—we'd be fools not to take advantage of it.'

The emotional strain was becoming too much for her. Wanting only to end the conversation, she said with brutal frankness, 'I can't even stand up to kiss you.'

'For God's sake! You're not listening to me. I've met any number of women since Annette and I split up, and not one of them was in a wheelchair and not one of them made the slightest impression on me.' He let go of her, staring moodily down the hillside. 'Don't tell me you've reacted with every other man you've met the way you reacted to me—because I won't believe you.'

'I told you I hadn't. I didn't know it could be like . . . . like it was,' she finished lamely.

Paul shot her a shrewd glance. 'But didn't I read in some newspaper or magazine rumours to the effect that you were about to get engaged? Some kind of business merger was involved, wasn't it?'

So he even knew about Philip . . . 'It was never official,' she said tersely. 'My family was all in favour of it, my father especially, because it did have business implications. Philip's family had the controlling interest in a company my father was interested in acquiring. And in Philip's eyes I was the only child of a very wealthy man.' There was no mistaking the cynicism in her voice. 'But after the accident no amount of money could persuade Philip to follow through with the engagement. My father was furious—with him for backing out and with me for being stupid enough to fall off the horse in the first place . . . so that's the story of my so-called engagement.'

'What's he like, this Philip?'

From the trees the thrush carolled its rich melodic song; it had been providing a counterpoint for this whole conversation, Meg realised. 'Tall, dark, and handsome,' she said glibly. But she could say the same of Paul Moreton, couldn't she, and Philip and Paul were as different as two men could be.

'The man was a fool. But I suppose you know that.'

There was an undertone of real anger in his voice that she did not understand. 'Maybe,' she said noncommittally. 'He certainly missed out on the chance for a lot of money.'

'That's not what I meant.'

'And before you ask the question, the answer's no—I never felt with him remotely the way I feel with you.'

'I knew that without asking.' Without changing his tone of voice, he said, 'Marry me, Meg.'

'No, Paul.'

'Somehow I'll make you change your mind.'

Her chin set stubbornly. 'You won't. There's no possible way you can.'

'We'll see about that.' He stood up and stretched lazily,

as if they were just concluding a casual, friendly chat. Bending down, he picked her up, and she discerned that whatever had anaesthetised her the past couple of weeks was gone: his hands seemed to burn through her clothing. As he carried her down the hillside, Meg held herself rigidly, certain from the faint smile on his lips that he knew exactly what was going on. They drove home in silence. When Paul left her on her doorstep he said, as if nothing had happened, 'See you tomorrow afternoon. 'Bye, Meg.' A mocking salute and he was striding up the path towards Ada's; before he got there she could hear him whistling.

Meg let herself into the shack. It was nearly seven o'clock, so she forced herself to prepare some kind of a meal and to eat it. She cleared it away and took out her embroidery for a while. But the threads snarled and knotted, and she made a mistake in the design and had to unpick it, so that in exasperation she finally gave up and went to bed. She lay on her back, staring up into the darkness, no longer able to ignore all that had happened that afternoon. Paul had asked her to marry him . . .

Alone with her thoughts, she knew that had she met him last year, she might well have said yes. But fate had been unkind enough to send him now, when she had no choice but to turn down his proposal. She could not marry anyone, least of all a man as virile and demanding as Paul Moreton. A tear trickled down her cheek, and then another, and it was some time before she eventually fell into a restless and troubled sleep.

CHAPTER FIVE

It was raining the next day, weather that exactly fitted Meg's mood. The only bright spot came from her realisation that Kevin was coming for his regular visit today, which gave her the perfect excuse not to go anywhere or do anything with Paul. If she had come to any conclusions last night, it had been that she dared not risk a repetition of their lovemaking on the hillside; it had seemed so beautiful and so right, and was so utterly wrong. There must be no more outings with only the two of them; in fact, at the moment, she winced away from the thought of spending time with him at all, for it could only be a constant reminder of all that she had lost in those few terrible seconds when the black horse had fallen across her legs . . .

Mid-morning there came a light tap at the door. Her nerves tightened uncomfortably. 'Oh, hi, Chris, how are you this morning?'

He was wearing his yellow raincoat, his dark hair plastered to his forehead. He grinned at her, and she saw a new gap in his teeth. 'It's raining.'

'I never would have guessed. Take your boots off and come on in. What are you up to this morning?'

'My father's working, Ada's scrubbing floors, Ben's out on the boat, so I came to see you.' From under his coat he produced a couple of books and from a pocket a box of crayons. 'I'm going to colour.'

She had noticed more than once how good he was at amusing himself, guessing that his mother must often have left him to his own devices. 'Do you want a cookie and a glass of milk?'

'Okay,' he said, adding as an obvious afterthought, 'thank you.'

They settled down companionably, Meg managing in no time to correct her mistakes of the night before. Her needle darted in and out, and she knew she would soon be able to finish this. 'That reminds me, Chris. When you go back up to Ada's, would you mind telling your father that I won't be able to go anywhere today? Kevin's coming.' It was a cowardly way out, getting Chris to act as her messenger, but she found in herself a strong aversion to even seeing Paul today.

'That's too bad. He said we might go to a movie 'cause it was raining.'

'I'm sure he'll take you, anyway.' She said tentatively, aware that it was a risk, 'He's a good father to you, Chris.'

The little boy dug the orange crayon into the paper. 'Mmmm.'

'I know he loves you.' More furious scrubbing of the paper with the crayon. She tried another tack. 'Do you like living here?'

A very different response. He smiled at her, looking momentarily so like his father that her breath caught in her throat. 'It's a great place! Me and Ben have lots of fun.'

'Ben and I,' she corrected automatically.

In the manner of small boys he ignored this. 'I like you, too,' he said naïvely, glancing at her from under his thick fringe of dark lashes.

She was taken unawares by a rush of such love for him that she had to put down her needlework, her vision too blurred to see what she was doing. 'Oh, Chris,' she said helplessly.

Perhaps it was the quiver in her voice or the softness in her face; Chris suddenly got up from his chair and catapulted himself into her lap. She hugged him fiercely, resting her cheek on his hair. His voice muffled in her sweater, she heard him say, 'I wish you were my mother.'

Her heart skipped a beat. She took a deep, steadying breath. 'You already have a mother, Chris.'

'She loves Oliver a lot more than me.'

Oliver . . . Annette's second husband. 'But she loves you, too.'

'She was hardly ever home. I was sick a lot, and she didn't like that. It got on her nerves.'

The last sentence could only have been a direct quote. Meg's arms tightened around the child. Foolish, self-centred Annette, to have had a husband like Paul and a son like Chris and to have thrown them both away. 'Do you miss her?'

'Nope,' he said phlegmatically. 'Not any more. I like you better.' His words were like an arrow straight to her heart. But worse was yet to come. 'If you 'n my father got married, then you'd be my mother, wouldn't you?'

'Your stepmother. But Chris, that isn't going to happen.'

He sat up straight. 'Why not?'

What reason could she give him that he would understand and accept? 'Your father and I don't love each other, Chris.'

'He thinks you're nice. I heard him say so to Ada.'

Oh, damn . . . 'But grown-ups don't get married just because they think someone's nice,' she said weakly.

'Very nice, he said.' His mouth set mutinously.

Paul Moreton should learn to keep his opinions to himself, she thought angrily, wondering how long Chris had been harbouring these thoughts. 'Apart from all that,' she said gently, 'I'm not going to marry anyone, Chris, because I have to stay in a wheelchair, you see.'

'So what?' he said rudely. But his lower lip was trembling, and there were tears hanging on his lashes.

Cut to the quick, wishing she was anywhere but where she was, she murmured, 'Chris, we'll be together all summer, and we can see each other every day. Let's enjoy what we have.'

He pulled free of her hold. Tears were pouring down his cheeks and dripping on his T-shirt. 'No! I want you to be my mother!' Before she could stop him he turned and ran for the door.

'Chris—come back!'

Not bothering with either his boots or his coat, his response was to slam the door behind him. Meg hurriedly steered herself to the window, and looked out of the rain-streaked glass. Chris was racing across the field and even as she watched, he tripped on a tussock of grass and fell. Picking himself up, he ran across Ada's lawn and disappeared into the house.

For several minutes Meg sat by the window staring unseeingly at the dismal view, hating her inability to run after him, castigating herself for handling the situation so poorly. She had hurt Chris, whom she loved . . . yet how could she have avoided it? She could not offer him hope where there was none, or make him false promises.

First the father, now the son. She felt emotionally battered, drained by the demands they had made on her; demands she could not possibly fulfil.

Fortunately Kevin came earlier than she had expected. 'I'm so glad to see you,' she said spontaneously. Then, as he looked rather surprised at the warmth of her welcome, she added lamely, 'It must be the weather—all this rain.'

'If you think this is bad, wait until the fall. You can get a whole week of days like this. I'll have to be sure to visit you then!'

'How are things going?' she asked, not at all in the mood for any kind of overtures from Kevin.

'Could hardly be better. Sales are well up compared with last year. I've added a line of pewter from the couple who live at Harrington Beach, and Peter Burroughs has given me half a dozen of his paintings. I figure it's a good idea to diversify as much as possible . . . How about you? I was talking to Ben one day at the store and he said you were out and about with your new neighbour quite a bit.'

Meg flushed. 'It was to keep his son company.'

'Really?'

'Really,' she said firmly. 'Do you want to see what I've been working on?'

Goodnaturedly he accepted her change of subject. 'Sure. I've got some new stuff for you, too. And I brought the account books from the store with me, Meg. If it's all right with you, I could work on them here. Maybe the weather was getting to me, too—I just didn't feel like staying at the store all afternoon, cooped up in the office.'

Within a few minutes they were settled at their respective tasks, Meg putting the finishing touches on the tablecloth, Kevin bent over the ledgers, a pocket calculator in his hand. When Paul burst unceremoniously in the door, it must have seemed a very peaceful scene—not that he looked in the mood to appreciate it.

His precipitate arrival startled Meg. Her needle slipped, digging into her finger, and she gave a tiny exclamation of pain. 'It's customary to knock,' she said coldly.

He leaned back against the door panels; it did not take long to see he was in a towering rage. 'I've come for Chris's boots and coat,' he said in a clipped voice.

Giving nothing away in her tone of voice, she answered, 'They're there by the door.'

He barely glanced at them. 'What the hell did you say to him to upset him so? He must have cried for nearly half an hour before he finally dropped off to sleep.'

Kevin said blandly, 'Good afternoon, Paul.'

'Afternoon. I asked you a question, Meg.'

There was no point in prevaricating. 'He said he wanted me to be his mother—to marry you. I said I couldn't. That was all.'

His breath hissed between his teeth. 'That was enough, I would have thought. Couldn't you have handled it a little less bluntly? So he didn't come running home crying his eyes out?'

That she herself had had similar doubts did not help matters at all. 'How, Paul? By fobbing him off with some kind of half-truth? Maybe, or perhaps or let's wait and see? Would you have preferred that I did that?'

'You could have said yes.'

She leaned forward in her chair, her blue eyes blazing. 'We went through all this yesterday. The answer was no for you, and it's the same for Chris. What did you do—send him over on purpose, Paul? A bit of emotional blackmail?'

In four long strides he had reached her chair and was shaking her by the shoulders. 'You know damn well I wouldn't do a thing like that!'

She knew he was right. 'I'm sorry——' she began.

He cut across her; in fact, she doubted if he even heard her. 'Chris came on his own initiative, because he loves you and he needs the security of being loved back. But you're so caught up in your own troubles you can't even recognise anyone else's needs.'

'That's not true!'

'Oh yes, it is!'

They had both raised their voices and had completely forgotten the third person in the room. Now Kevin said apologetically, 'Ada's coming down the path. Unless you want her to hear you screaming like a couple of banshees, I think you'd better cool it.'

Meg's anger subsided so abruptly that she had to swallow an hysterical urge to giggle. 'I wonder what she wants,' she said inanely.

A polite tap at the door and Ada walked in. Paul had released Meg and now he straightened slowly. 'Is Chris okay?'

Ada looked at them both in equal disapprobation, and Meg was sure she must have overheard some of their quarrel; Ada did not approve of the more violent emotions, particularly in a woman. 'The boy's fine. Ben wants to take him to the supply store to get lobster twine, so he'll need his coat and boots.'

'I was just going to bring them up, Ada,' said Paul with a meekness that even in the circumstances amused Meg.

Ada looked him straight in the eye, not yielding an inch. 'It didn't sound like that to me.'

Wickedly Meg intervened. 'But he'll take them up now. Won't you, Paul?'

'I will.' He glared at her. 'And as I hadn't finished what I wanted to say, we'll carry on with this conversation at another time.' He nodded curtly at Kevin, gathered up Chris's clothes and held the door open for Ada. With exaggerated politeness he closed it very quietly behind him.

Meg let out her breath in a long sigh in time to hear Kevin say, 'Well, it's certainly rarely dull around here since that guy came. I'm beginning to think Kathy and I have an idyllic relationship. Asked you to marry him, did he?'

'Yes, he did, and if you breathe that to another living soul, I'll have your head, Kevin Langley!'

Piously he crossed his hands over the approximate region of his heart. 'My lips are sealed,' he intoned.

'They'd better be.' Then, 'Oh, Kevin, it's such a mess!'

'I gather you turned him down?'

She banged the metal rims on the wheelchair with her clenched fists, a gesture that said more than words. 'What else could I do?'

Kevin had never directly alluded to her inability to walk, and she suspected that under his somewhat pugnacious exterior he was too softhearted to do so. Now all he said was, 'He must like you as you are or he wouldn't ask you to marry him.'

'He wants a mother for Chris, and he thinks I fill the bill—that's all it is. Don't get any ideas of a passionate romance going on in front of your eyes.'

'He looked pretty passionate to me a few minutes ago.'

'I have a feeling he's used to getting his own way,' she said wryly. 'But this is one time he's not going to.'

'Don't you think it would work out, Meg? A marriage, I mean,' Kevin persisted.

'I know it wouldn't. Oh, right now they both think I'm just what they need. But how long before I'd start to get in the way? I can't walk or run or dance or play ball— after a while I know they'd resent all that.'

There was complete conviction in her voice, but just the same Kevin said slowly, 'I'm not sure you're right, you know. I think you should give it a try, Meg.'

She had not expected Kevin to champion Paul's cause. 'You can't give marriage a try, Kevin,' she said shortly. 'You either do it wholeheartedly or you don't do it at all. And in my case, it's the latter.'

He tugged thoughtfully at his beard. 'He doesn't look the type to give up easily.'

'He hasn't got much choice. I just wish it hadn't happened, Kevin—we were doing fine as we were, and I

was really enjoying getting out so much. Now even that's
ruined.'

'If you enjoyed it that much, why should you enjoy it
less when you're married?'

'I'm beginning to think you *want* me married off,' she
said peevishly.

'I'd like you to be happy, Meg.'

He was so obviously sincere that she felt ashamed of
herself. 'That's sweet of you, Kevin. I *was* happy before
they came.' She sighed. 'Let's talk about something else.
How about a cup of tea?'

Neither Paul nor Chris came back that day. Kevin stayed
for supper, finished his accounts, played his guitar for her,
and left around ten. Meg went to bed shortly afterwards
and eventually fell asleep to the patter of rain on the roof
and the monotonous drip of water from the eaves.

The island was too small for Paul and Chris to avoid Meg
altogether, but after three days had passed in which Meg
had done no more than wave to them from a distance,
she concluded unhappily that they were managing it fairly
well. The island was also too small for such avoidance to
occur without Ben and Ada noticing it. Ada's sole comment, one morning when she brought back Meg's clean
washing, was a sharp sniff and a, 'Too bad people can't
get along in a place this size—what did you do to Chris to
hurt his feelings so?' Without waiting for an answer she
stalked back up the hill, disapproval radiating from every
inch of her rigid spine.

As if her visit had been a signal, fifteen minutes later
Ben wandered down the hill; he, however, was a little
more circumspect. Busily engaged in stuffing tobacco into
his pipe, he said, 'Chris is a bit off his feed these days.
And he didn't even want to go collecting mussels this
morning. Any idea what's wrong, lass?'

If Ben didn't know, it meant neither Paul nor Chris
had told him; nor would she, for it would only upset him
unnecessarily. 'We had an argument, Grandpa,' she said
evasively. 'They'll get over it.'

His shrewd blue eyes noticed the restless movements of

her hands among her embroidery silks. 'What was the argument about?'

'Why don't you ask Paul that?'

'I already did. He told me to ask you.'

'It's nothing important—it'll blow over.'

'I hope so, Meg. You were looking so well for a while, and it did my heart good to see you getting out and about every day. Not in love with him, are you?'

'No, Grandpa—stop being such an incurable romantic,' she said firmly.

'He'd make you a fine husband,' Ben said wistfully.

If one more person told her that, she'd start to scream. 'I daresay. How many lobsters did you and Randall get yesterday?'

'Nigh on two hundred pounds.' He had been searching in his pockets and said now, 'Must have left my matches up at the house—so I'll be on my way. You know where I am, lass, if you need anything.'

It was his way of offering her comfort and support; he had not been deceived by her evasive answers. 'Thanks, Grandpa.' He ambled off, still absentmindedly looking for his matches.

The clouds had been gathering all morning and Meg felt the first drops of rain on her bare arms—time to go in. Determined not to surrender to the depression and loneliness that seemed to be hovering over her, she turned on the radio and began to work, deliberately starting on a new design that would require her full attention.

Her next visitor was Paul. He knocked and, without waiting for her to answer, walked in. He stood in the doorway, his oilskin jacket shiny with rain; in an Aran pullover and dark cords tucked into fisherman's boots, he looked very large, very masculine, and very sure of himself. Also, she thought crossly, devastatingly handsome. And this was the man, she realised with a faint, unexpected jolt of wonder, who had asked her to marry . . .

'Hello,' was all she could find to say.

He acknowledged her greeting with a curt nod. 'I want you to do me a favour,' he said abruptly. 'Chris has been like a bear the last three days, and now it's raining again and he's complaining there's nothing to do. There's a matinee performance of a Walt Disney movie in Halifax. Will you go in with us?'

No 'please', she noticed. And if she said no, he would simply turn on his heel and leave—and probably go without her. Thinking with lightning speed, she recognised how impossible it was going to be for the three of them to continue avoiding each other for the whole summer; some kind of a compromise had to be reached, and they might as well make a start now. Besides which, she had missed Chris the past three days; missed him with an acuteness that had frightened her. 'All right,' she said composedly.

He showed no visible reaction to her decision. 'I'll pick you up in half an hour.'

In a conscious effort to raise her morale, Meg changed into a pale blue cotton dress that flattered her tanned skin and accentuated the blue of her eyes; she applied rather more make-up and perfume than usual; and brushed her hair until it fell in a shining curtain to her shoulders. She was adjusting her raincape around her shoulders when Paul came for her. 'Chris is waiting in the car,' he said, apparently not even noticing her appearance. 'Ready?'

Piqued, and then annoyed with herself for even caring whether or not Paul thought she looked nice, she merely nodded. Paul took the handles of her chair and steered her outdoors. As was always the way on wet days, the air was laden with the odours of seaweed and dead fish and salt water, while the far shore of the cove was blurred by the rain; as they crossed the bridge, the tide lapped and sucked at the pylons, and gurgled among the rocks. When Paul lifted her into the car, Meg held herself tensely, avoiding his eyes. Chris was sitting in the middle of the seat. He grinned at her shamefacedly. ''lo, Meg.'

'Hi, Chris.' She patted his knee quickly. 'Nice to see you. Are you looking forward to the movie?'

'Yeah. It's the one about the dogs. Dal . . . dal . . .'

'Dalmatians,' Meg said obligingly.

'Mmm . . . that's what I was going to say.'

As they drove to Halifax, Meg was glad to see that relations between her and Chris seemed to be more or less back to normal, although perhaps he was a shade less spontaneous, particularly when it came to physical contact. But she could not say the same about her relationship with Paul. He was polite and he spoke to her often enough that she could not accuse him of neglecting her; but the carefree exchanges of opinions and the jokes and laughter were gone, and with them the nebulous spark that had bound them together.

The movie was a welcome distraction; afterwards they took Chris to McDonald's, which was his idea of the epitome of dining out. On the way home he fell asleep, his silky head leaning against Meg's arm, a blob of ketchup on his chin. With the boy asleep, Paul no longer bothered to keep up any pretence of conversation between him and Meg, and the constraint and distance lay between them, virtually unbridgeable. With those other sundrenched afternoons fresh in her memory, it was doubly hard for Meg to bear; it would have been better, she thought numbly, if they had never become friends, if she had not allowed herself to be beguiled into that transitory closeness . . .

Once they got back to the island, she had Paul leave her up at Ben's, and made her own way down to the shack, Chris's ''Bye, Meg. See you tomorrow,' still echoing in her ears. But it was Paul who occupied her thoughts as she made herself a cup of tea and tried to read. She was not really surprised when tears began dripping down on the page, for she had been carrying the hurt all afternoon and it was pointless to keep it bottled up any longer. She cried for a while, quietly, although if anyone had asked her why she was crying, she would have found it difficult to answer; then, feeling better, she changed into a long silk robe and settled down to read in earnest.

She had certainly not expected any other visitors that night. Dusk was falling when she suddenly looked up from her book, frowning slightly. Wasn't that the sound of footsteps? Something authoritative in the rat-tat on the door panels told her instinctively that it was Paul. She sat up a little straighter in her chair. 'Come in.'

It *was* Paul. In silence he stepped out of his rubber

boots and hung up his jacket, then came closer into the circle of light thrown by her reading lamp. His hair had curled in the dampness, and he was staring at her in a way that made her feel uncomfortable. She had no idea of how beautiful she looked. She had pulled her hair back into a chignon, a simple and severe style that emphasised her high cheekbones and wide forehead; her long robe fell about her in shimmering folds of kingfisher blue, its mandarin collar and wide sleeves edged with rich gold and blue braid.

Paul continued to stare at her and her heart began to pound in her breast. She raised her chin defiantly, demanding, 'What do you want?'

His eyes lazily surveyed her from head to foot and their message was clear. A flush of delicate pink irradiated her cheeks, and still he did not speak. Pride, or stubbornness, or a combination of both, refused to allow her to drop her eyes, and in the end it was he who broke the silence. 'I've never seen you look more beautiful.'

Although her breast rose and fell in agitation, her eyes never wavered from his. 'You didn't come down here to tell me that.'

'No . . .' He pulled up a chair and straddled it, resting his hands and chin on the back, watching her sombrely. 'I came to ask you to reconsider, Meg . . . my offer of marriage, I mean. The last three days have been a disaster, and just what I didn't want to happen *has* happened—Chris has been hurt. For his sake, Meg, won't you please marry me, so that he can at least have a normal family life?'

That word 'normal' again . . . 'Normal is exactly what it wouldn't be——'

'Yes, it would. He already regards you as a mother. That's all he wants—a mother and father, like the rest of the boys he knows.'

For a moment she wavered. Kevin had urged her to marry Paul, wanting to see her happy. Ben had said Paul would make her a fine husband. Ada would be delighted with the match. And Chris . . . with a lump in her throat Meg fought back the image of how happy Chris would be. As for Paul, he would be pleased for Chris's sake, there could be no doubt about that; beyond that she could not go, because his own feelings were an enigma to her. Except, she remembered with a shiver of her nerves, that he desired her ...

As if he sensed her doubts, he said quietly, 'I'd look after you, Meg—you'd never want for anything.'

Except love, she thought dazedly. But then had not her accident permanently robbed her of that? She suddenly buried her face in her hands.

Swiftly he got up from his chair and knelt beside her. 'Don't, Meg. I didn't mean to upset you.'

A tear streaked between her fingers, for something in his steady gaze had made her realise that had things been different, she might well have taken her chances and married him; on the basis of the laughter and closeness they had shared, risked putting her happiness in his hands.

'Don't cry, Meg. Please, dear, don't cry.'

His gentleness and his endearment, the first he had ever used with her, affected her more powerfully than any of his other demands; when she felt him lift her in his arms and press her face into his chest, she offered no resistance. For a few brief moments it was sheer heaven to surrender to him, to give up all her cherished pride and independence ... Dimly she became aware that Paul was dropping kisses on her hair and on her forehead. She felt the first touch of panic and raised her head to protest.

With a muffled exclamation he kissed her full on the mouth, the touch of his lips like fire. His hands were moulding her body and she knew he must be aware of her nakedness under the silk robe. All the latent passion of her nature rose up to meet him and with every ounce of her will power she fought it back. She had surrendered to him once, and could not risk again being swept into submission by the sureness of his mouth and the fierce demands of his hands and body. She beat at his chest with her fists, and wrenched her mouth free. 'Don't, Paul! Put me down——'

His answer was to put her on the bed where she lay in

a tumble of blue silk, her fine-boned ankles and feet bare, her eyes brilliant with mingled fear and rage. Then he was beside her and to her furious, 'Leave me alone!' he groaned, 'I want you, Meg—don't fight me.'

She had to . . . as his hand found the swell of her breast through the thin fabric, she knew how easily he could make her lose all sanity and reason. She mustn't let it happen again, for she could not bear it. Frantic with fear, she screamed, 'Let go, Paul!' Somehow the flat of her hand connected with his jaw, the force of her blow sending a shooting pain up her wrist.

And then, from nowhere, a small body hurtled on to the bed, and a shrill voice cried hysterically, 'You're hurting Meg! Let go! Let go, you mustn't hurt Meg. I hate you, I hate you!'

Paul rolled over, grabbing Chris by the shoulders and trying to avoid the hail of blows from the boy's fists. 'Chris! What are you doing here?'

'I hate you! You were hurting Meg, and it was all because of you that I had to go to the hospital and they hurt me too!'

Meg knew she was forgotten. She sat up, seeing how Paul's big body had frozen to stillness, how he was not even aware of Chris still pummelling his chest and arms, for his whole attention was focussed on the stream of words that were erupting from his son. 'You took me away from home and put me in that hospital. It was all your fault I had the operation and all those needles, and the doctor said it wouldn't hurt and it did—you're mean and I hate you!'

'Chris, it wasn't like that. Oh, son . . .'

Chris was sobbing now, his vision blinded by tears. Paul let go of him, reaching in his pocket for a handkerchief. 'Here,' he said gently, 'let me wipe your eyes. I can explain it all, Chris.'

But Chris was beyond reason. He struck out at his father's hand, scrambled to the floor and ran for the door. There was the hollow echo of his steps across the ramp and then only the steady thrumming of the rain on the roof.

CHAPTER SIX

PAUL had been sitting on the edge of the bed, and now he turned a face to Meg that was blank with shock. 'We explained it all so carefully to him, myself and the doctors. I thought he understood, but I don't think he could have heard a word we said.' He raked his fingers through his hair. 'All this time he was blaming me for the operation— no wonder he hated me!'

'But now that he's said all that, maybe you'll be able to straighten it out between you. You'd better go after him.'

Paul stood up very slowly. 'Yes. Will you be all right?'

'Just bring my chair over by the bed in case I need it.'

He did as she asked and then said, 'I'll let you know what happens, Meg. Who knows, maybe this will have been just the breakthrough we needed.' Moving like a man in a dream, he pulled on his oilskin jacket and rubber boots and followed Chris out of the door.

For several minutes Meg stayed where she was, her mind in a whirl as she relived Paul's proposal, her terrified reaction to his lovemaking, and Chris's total loss of control; she did hope that this would mean that he and Paul could work out their differences. Too restless to contemplate going to bed now, she got up and put on the kettle, her usual panacea when she could not sleep. She had made the tea and was getting the milk out of the refrigerator when her door was flung open. It was Paul.

'Did Chris come back here?'

She felt her heart clench in fear. 'No—I haven't seen him. Can't you find him?'

'No. He's not at Ada's or Ben's, or in the toolshed or down at the wharf. Can you think where he might have gone?'

Meg forced back a wave of sheer panic and deliberately tried to concentrate. 'He's always loved going to the little beach and to the lighthouse. But he wouldn't be able to find his way in the dark, would he?' She had a sudden nightmare vision of the surf pounding on the rocks below the lighthouse, and briefly closed her eyes. Surely Chris wouldn't have gone out there, not alone ... but he had been so upset when he left, he could have gone anywhere.

'Ben and I'll go out there now. Would you go up by Ada's, and call him? He might come for you where he wouldn't for me.'

'Of course. I'll get dressed and go right away. And Paul—good luck.'

'Thanks.' He nodded at her and was gone.

She dressed in record time, pulling on her raincape and dropping a poncho over her knees. Taking a torch from the cupboard under the sink, she wheeled herself out-doors.

It was pitch black. The wind had come up, driving the rain into her face like pellets; over its wailing, she could hear the distant roar of the sea. Trying not to think of Chris out alone in this, praying that he was safe, she balanced the flashlight in her lap and headed for Ada's. Every light was on in both the other houses. Meg began to call Chris's name, sweeping the torch in a semi-circle to light up the shed and the bushes, and suppressing a shriek of alarm as Ada emerged from behind the corner of Ben's house, a witch-like figure in her long black raincape. 'Any sign of him, Ada?' Meg called, knowing in advance from the expression on Ada's face what the answer would be.

'None. He never came back to the house at all.'

'Why did he come down in the first place?'

'There was a long-distance phone call for his father. I waited as long as I could, then told them to call back later. I thought of going to look for Chris ... if only I had, I might have seen which way he went—towards the lighthouse or over the bridge.'

Meg thought of the winding road edged by bogs and tidal inlets, and said desperately, 'Surely he wouldn't have left the island?' Again she raised her voice. 'Chris! Chri-is!'

'Paul said if he and Ben couldn't find him on the island, we'd call the police. You'd better go inside, Meg, there's no point in staying out here and getting soaked. I'm going to make up a bed by the fire and get the hot water bottles out.'

'I'll stay here for a while,' Meg said stubbornly. 'I told Paul I'd keep calling Chris.'

Ada clucked her tongue in disapproval and went indoors. Meg steered herself back and forth across the wet grass, calling in all directions, cupping her cold hands around her mouth to give her voice greater volume. But the ground she could cover was of necessity limited; bushes, rocks, and the steep hill to the bridge kept her confined to an area around the three houses. Not since the day by the beach had she felt so sharply the limitations of her disability: Chris was lost and all she could do was go round in circles calling his name.

Finally she caught through the trees the glimmer of a torch, its beam sweeping from side to side. 'Paul? Ben? Did you find him?'

It was Paul's deep voice that overrode the wind and the rain. 'No, no sign of him. Ben's coming back along the shore. You'd better come inside, Meg—I'm going to call the police and then go looking for him in the car.'

This time she obeyed, for sheer logic told her that by now Chris must be out of earshot. Ada had turned the furnace up and had lit the woodstove in the kitchen; both kettles were simmering, while there were three hot water bottles and fresh sheets on the couch. After one look at Meg, Ada said, 'Take off your rain gear and then come by the fire—your hair's soaked.'

She was wet, although not half as wet as Chris must be by now; she fought down the whole series of nightmare images that this thought evoked. From the other room she could hear the low murmur of Paul's voice, and knew he was contacting the police. It seemed to be a long conversation, for it was five minutes before he came back in the room. 'It'll take an hour and a half for them to get here,' he said. 'They're bringing a tracking dog with them, so they have to come from Halifax. He doesn't want us to go on foot searching the area across the bridge, because it only confuses the dog. So there's nothing to do but wait until they come.' He stared down at his hands as if he had never seen them before, his mind obviously a long way away. 'I'm going to take the car, though, and go along the road a little way—I'll be back before the police get here.'

'Drive carefully, Paul.'

'I will.' All his movements seemed to have slowed, and he rummaged in his pockets for his car keys, his eyes on a pair of Chris's shoes that had been left by the stove; they were scuffed and muddy and looked very small beside his own big boots. Meg felt her heart ache with compassion for him as his hands lingered briefly on the scuffed, diminutive shoes. 'You'll stay here, will you, Meg? I'd like you to be here if we—when we bring him back.'

'Of course you'll be bringing him back,' she said, putting all the conviction she could into her voice. 'And of course I'll be here.'

'Good girl!' Small words, but they warmed her heart. Paul finally found his car keys and went outdoors again.

Later, when Meg recalled that evening, it was the waiting that she remembered—the interminable, anxious waiting. Time seemed to have slowed down, for she would glance at the clock and then, what seemed like aeons later, look again, to find that only two or three minutes had passed. Ada bustled around, keeping herself busy; Ben was still presumably searching the shoreline; for Meg there was nothing to do but wait—and worry.

Ben was the first one to arrive back. He stamped into the back porch, where Ada fussed around him, hanging up his wet clothes and for once making no remarks about the tracks on her spotless floors. 'Come in by the fire, Ben. Pull up the rocker now and get out of those wet socks.'

Ben sank down into the chair, drying his face with the towel Ada had given him; he looked exhausted. 'Not a sign of the boy. Between us, Paul and I covered every inch of the island.' Gratefully he accepted a mug of steaming, well-sugared tea from Ada. 'All along I tried to teach Chris a healthy respect for the ocean, so we can only hope he heeded me, and didn't go out on the rocks—there's a high sea running. Are the police coming?'

Meg quickly brought him up to date. Three-quarters of an hour later Paul came in, and after one look at his drawn face Meg didn't bother asking any questions. 'I went along every road in the area—over to the village and as far as South Point,' he volunteered. 'Blew the horn the whole way—not a sign of him.' Restlessly he paced up and down, refusing Ada's offer of tea. 'He'll be wet through. One of the things the doctor in Toronto warned me against was letting him get chilled. Which reminds me—I'd better phone the local doctor.'

Meg could tell how badly the waiting was chafing on his nerves. She went over to the window and stared out into the darkness; although the outside light was on, everything was distorted by the rain streaming down the windowpane. Behind her the rocking chair creaked as Ben rocked back and forth. Paul had begun pacing up and down, up and down, until she felt as though she would scream from the tension. Then, at last, across the bridge she saw the rhythmic red flash of the lights of the police car. 'They're here,' she said.

Paul grabbed his jacket. 'I'll go and meet them.'

From her stance by the window she watched him run across the grass. In a few minutes he was back, accompanied by two men, heads bent against the wind, and a large black and tan Alsatian who loped at their sides. The kitchen seemed to shrink as the three men came in, and a considerable amount more damage was done to Ada's floor. The dogmaster was the shorter of the two policemen; he had sandy-coloured hair cropped close to his head and a broad, blunt-featured face which exuded calmness and competence. Smiling reassuringly at Meg, he said, 'Mrs Moreton? I'm Roger Shaw.'

She flushed. 'I'm a friend of Mr Moreton's.'

'Chris's mother doesn't live with me any more,' Paul interjected.

Roger Shaw showed no visible reaction to this. 'I see. Can you tell me what happened, Mr Moreton? Chris is how old?'

'Five.'

'You said something about your son running away?'

Briefly Paul described the change in custody from Annette to himself, Chris's hospitalisation and operation, and tonight's violent outburst. 'We've searched the island from one end to the other,' he concluded. 'I think he must have gone across the bridge.'

'And no one's looked over there?'

'No—you said specifically that we shouldn't.'

'Good—you'd be surprised how many people disregard that. Then you get a whole mess of fresh tracks and it makes it twice as difficult for the dog. I'll bring Major in now—he's had time to stretch his legs after the car journey.' He returned with the dog pacing sedately at his heels. 'Now, where can I find something that Chris has worn recently?'

'His shoes are there by the stove. His clothes are upstairs.'

When they came back down Roger Shaw was carrying Chris's sweater; he put a leather harness on the dog and then let him sniff the sweater thoroughly, talking to him in a low voice and repeating a word that sounded to Meg like 'soo'. He must have caught her look of perplexity, for he said in explanation, 'It's a German command, "*zu*"— I'm telling Major he's got to track Chris down. Okay, we're going to leave now. It might take a while to pick up the trail on the other side of the bridge, because the rain makes it harder.' He glanced over at the other, younger policeman. 'Mike, give me a few minutes, then wait in the car.' He patted his pocket radio in his navy jacket. 'I'll call in when I've found Chris.'

When, not if, Meg noticed, comforted by Shaw's businesslike manner and by the obvious rapport that existed between master and dog. But he was still talking. 'Mr Moreton, by all means wait with Mike in the car. Major and I have to do the search alone, because another strange scent only confuses him. But I'll be in touch with Mike just as soon as I find Chris.'

'Thanks,' Paul said soberly, his smile not reaching his eyes. 'Good luck.'

Silence descended on the remaining people in the kitchen. Paul began pacing back and forth again; Meg knew he was hating the enforced inactivity, but was intelligent enough to realise that the search was being conducted in the best possible way, and that his presence would only have been a hindrance.

After fifteen minutes or so, Mike, who had been outside, came back in and reported, 'They've set off down the road, so they must have picked up the trail. We could go out and wait in the car now, sir.'

Paul turned to Meg. 'Do you want to come with us?'

'Yes, please,' she answered simply, touched that he had thought to ask her when his whole mind must be occupied by concern for his son.

Paul carried her to the car. They all sat in the front seat, listening to the static and the intermittent messages on the short-wave radio. Time passed. It was nearly an hour later that Roger Shaw's exuberant voice came across the air. 'Found him! And he's in good shape. I'm taking a bearing, Mike. I should be out in twenty minutes or so. Meet me about a quarter of a mile up the road.'

'Thank God,' Paul said quietly. He put an arm around Meg's shoulders and drew her close, as if wanting to share his intense relief with her. Because it seemed the right thing to do, she reached up and kissed him on the cheek, feeling the roughness of his beard under her lips. He smiled down at her, and for a brief, tangible moment they experienced a closeness, a complete sharing of emotion, such as Meg had never felt before, and that left her shaken.

She was brought sharply back to earth when Mike pressed a button and over their heads the siren wailed into the night. 'Helps Roger get his bearings,' he explained, as he drove slowly down the road. Three more times he sounded the siren and as the last note died away the dogmaster's figure suddenly appeared beside the car, a wet and bedraggled Major at his heels, Chris almost totally covered by his jacket.

Paul opened the door and Roger Shaw leaned down, transferring Chris into Paul's arms. The boy seemed to have been drowsing. His eyes fluttered open and the first person he saw was his father. 'Dad?' he whimpered.

It was the word Meg had never heard him use before. Her vision was obscured by tears as Paul wordlessly held out his arms and Chris was put into them, burrowing his wet head into his father's sweater. Paul held him close, his head bent, his eyes closed.

In the meantime Roger Shaw had opened the back door and Major had jumped up on the seat, followed by his master. Mike drove on until he found a widening in the road where he could turn around. Then Meg heard Chris say, 'I was lost—it was scary. But the dog found me. Can we get one of those dogs, Dad?'

'When we find a place to live, maybe we could.'

'His name's Major. I'm sorry I ran away, Dad.'

'I'm sorry, too—it's not usually the best way to sort things out. But I'm glad we found you.'

'Yeah . . .' Chris settled himself more comfortably in Paul's arms and his eyes drooped shut again. 'The dog licked my face. If we got one, he could sleep on my bed.'

There was a thread of laughter in Paul's voice. 'We'd have to see about that.' But his son was asleep.

From the back seat Roger Shaw said, 'The rain was the worst problem. Major lost the scent a couple of times and we had to circle to pick it up again. Chris hadn't really gone that far, but I could have walked right past him and not even have seen him—he was curled up under a spruce, fast asleep. But Major led me right to him.'

Meg had been looking back over her shoulder as the policeman talked. At the mention of his name, Major pricked up his ears, his brown eyes expressive of intelligence and what seemed like an almost human comprehension. Shaw removed the dog's harness and put it on the seat beside the long lead he had been carrying. 'He's a good dog, isn't he? Good dog!' A wet tail thumped against the seat.

Back at the house all was confusion. The doctor had arrived, so he, Paul and Chris stayed in the warmth of the kitchen, while Ada ushered the rest of them into the parlour, where she plied them all with tea and cookies and rich chocolate cake. She had even allowed Major in the parlour; he flopped down on the floor beside the dogmaster's chair and rested his head on his paws. Soon afterwards the doctor and Paul joined them, according to the former there was little danger of any permanent damage to the boy. Finally, in a flurry of thanks and goodbyes, the two police officers and Major left.

Paul was going to stay downstairs with Chris, and as Ada started bringing in more bedding, Meg suddenly realised how tired she was. 'Time I went home. Thanks for the tea, Ada.'

'I'll go down with you,' Ben offered, smothering a huge yawn.

Chris was already asleep, and to Meg's, 'Goodnight, Paul,' there came only an abstracted, 'Goodnight, Meg. See you tomorrow.' Feeling strangely deflated after all the excitement, Meg allowed Ben to wheel her down to the shack. 'Sleep well, lass,' he said gruffly.

'You, too, Grandpa.'

Once inside, she added a couple of logs to the fire, and got undressed and into bed in record time. Her last thoughts were of sheer gratitude that Chris was safe and that somehow, through his outburst of anger and his lonely trek through the rain, he had found his way to his father.

That this was so was reinforced for her the next afternoon when Chris came for a visit. He looked very little the worse for his ordeal, she was glad to see. 'I slept until noon,' he boasted. 'And Ada made me blueberry muffins for my breakfast, 'cause they're my favourites. Dad was still asleep when I woke up, so I went and jumped on him and we had a wrestle. He's going to take me trout fishing tomorrow. Ben's going to lend us fishing rods.'

'That sounds like fun.'

'We're going to dig up worms tonight, Dad and me, in Ben's garden, and keep them in a can.' He added with gusto, 'Dad's going to show me how to put them on the hook.'

Dad this and Dad that . . . 'It sounds as though you're.

feeling pretty good about your father,' commented Meg.

'Yeah . . .' He hung his head. 'It wasn't his fault I had to go to the hospital—it was because I was sick. And I'm better now, I can do all kinds of things I wasn't allowed to before.'

'I'm glad, Chris.'

It was plainly impossible for Chris to remain repentant for long. 'Me too!' He grinned at her, a gap-toothed grin that did funny things to her heart. 'It would be neat if Dad 'n me got a dog like Major, wouldn't it?' He burbled on contentedly for another few minutes, then left to go in search of his father. Shortly afterwards Meg noticed them walking hand in hand down the slope that led to the bridge.

She sat still for some time after they were out of sight, her hands idle in her lap, torn between all sorts of contradictory emotions. She was happy that Chris and Paul were reconciled, for she knew how much Paul had suffered from his son's aloofness; yet she was honest enough with herself to admit that one of the consequences of their new closeness was that she herself felt left out. Redundant. Chris would not need her nearly as much now that he had his father, nor would Paul need her to act as a buffer between him and his son, to give the impression of a family warmth. She did not think he would repeat his offer of marriage.

Which was just as well, she thought crossly, trying to quell the hollow feeling that seemed to have lodged itself somewhere in the vicinity of her midriff. Because she had now, and never had had, any intention of marrying him; if anything, the episode of Chris's disappearance had only served to re-emphasise her dependence on her wheelchair and her helplessness. There was no future in the relationship with Paul and Chris, she had known that from the start. So why was she feeling so unhappy?

Four days passed. She had brief visits from Chris and Paul, but they were plainly so absorbed in each other's company that she wondered, with a bitterness that startled her by its intensity, why they bothered. She did learn from them that on Monday they were flying up to Toronto for Chris's check-up with the heart surgeon, which happened to be the same day for her monthly appointment with the specialist in Halifax. She was almost glad that they were going; she sensed that she would feel less lonely knowing they were two thousand miles away than when they were just up the hill.

As an antidote to her mental confusion, she threw herself into the various projects she was working on for Kevin; the tourist season was in full swing, and she knew he would take everything she did. So it was that on Sunday afternoon, when Paul arrived, she was sitting by the window that overlooked the sea, her attention focused on her needlework rather than on the play of sunshine on the rippling waters of the cove.

It was characteristic of Paul to come straight to the point. 'What in the world are you doing indoors on a beautiful day like this?'

Not a propitious beginning. 'What does it look like?'

'Like you're ruining your eyesight.'

That she had been overstraining her eyes did not improve her temper. 'I'm a big girl now, Paul—and they're my eyes.'

His mouth thinned in exasperation. 'I sometimes think you're the most aggravating female I've ever known. Put that stuff away—we're going out.'

'Maybe I don't want to.'

'And stop holding the needle as though you want to jab me with it. I don't care whether you want to go out or not. We're going anyway.'

'Where's Chris?' Meg demanded, thinking to distract him.

'Ada has permitted Ben to take her and Chris over to the Point to visit some of her numerous grandchildren. Ben's in seventh heaven, of course, and it'll be good for Chris to play with some kids his own age. So come on.'

'You're sure you can spare the time? To be with me, I mean,' she said, then could have bitten off her tongue in vexation for letting him know that she had noticed his absence the past few days.

Something flared in his eyes. 'So you're not quite as

uninterested as you appear to be,' he said softly. 'Neither one of us has seen much of you the last few days, Meg. It seemed important that Chris and I be together a lot—to cement things, as it were. So you missed me, did you?'

'No!' she snapped. 'It was Chris I missed.'

'I'm not sure I believe you.' He took the handles of her chair and steered it towards the door. 'We'll continue this outdoors. You need a bit of colour in your cheeks—you look like a ghost.'

Infuriated as much by his unflattering description of her looks as by his high-handed attitude, she retorted untruthfully, 'I wish you'd just leave me alone.'

Paul ignored her. They went up the slope and behind Ben's house to the path that led to the lighthouse, Meg sitting bolt upright, no longer pale as a ghost because of the spots of angry colour in her cheeks. But it took nearly half an hour to reach the lighthouse, for Paul was in no hurry. He stopped two or three times so they could watch the antics of a couple of rabbits in the underbrush; so Meg could admire a cluster of ragged purple orchids growing in a damp hollow in the ground and see a pair of terns diving for fish in the cove. Imperceptibly the summer afternoon began to weave its spell around the girl. She forgot that she was angry with Paul and began to enjoy herself, drinking in all the myriad sights and scents that the island had to offer. She had never been as far as the lighthouse before, having only seen it from the deck of *Harriet III*. Its tower was white with a red roof and a huge glass eye, the whole structure anchored to the bare rock in the clearing at the seaward tip of the island. Beyond stretched the vast blue waters of the Atlantic.

Paul carried her to the edge of the grass and sat down beside her, apparently content to gaze in silence at the ever-shifting patterns of light and shadow on the ocean's surface. Ten feet below them the smooth waves reared up and struck the rocks and dissolved into hissing white foam. In the end it was Meg who spoke. 'How lovely it is here,' she said dreamily. 'You know, a year ago I'd never have taken the time to sit like this and simply look at the sea— I always had to be on the go. I'm beginning to think that

I missed a lot in those days.'

He smiled at her, and she noticed how close to her he was sitting; his teeth were very white against his tanned skin, his eyes pools of darkness. She wondered if he was going to kiss her, and in her bones knew she would be unable to offer any resistance if he did. More than that—she wanted him to kiss her, wanted his arms to go around her, his hands to relearn the contours of her body.

From a long way away, as if from another world, came the haunting, melancholy cry of a seagull. His smile had faded, and when he spoke it was as if he had erased every trace of emotion from his voice. 'Do you know why I brought you out here?'

'No—why?' Her heart began to bang against her ribs, and unconsciously her fingers pulled at the grass.

'To try once more to persuade you, one way or another, to marry me.'

'Paul, we've been through all that——'

'We have, haven't we? Do I keep coming back because you keep saying no?'

'Perhaps it's a novel experience for you.'

'You're right there,' he said with some feeling. 'Or is it because of your clear blue eyes that seem to look right through me? Or your stubborn little chin that asks no quarter? I often wonder if it's not that you're the exact opposite to Annette—she couldn't even work a can-opener on her own. Whereas you, since your accident, have managed to make a whole new life for yourself, to keep busy and independent ... hell, I don't know, Meg.' He ran his fingers through her hair, his eyes gazing unseeingly at the far horizon. 'I had it all planned when I came to get you this afternoon. We've got the island to ourselves and I was going to bring you out here and seduce you— make love to you until you'd say yes rather than no.' He grimaced. 'Don't look so scared—I suddenly find I can't do it to you, much as I'd like to. Paul Moreton, the perfect gentleman. Perfect fool, more like ... it would have worked, wouldn't it, Meg?'

'Probably,' she said evenly, knowing it was useless to

try and deny the effect he had on her.

There was torment in the dark eyes that roamed over her face, lingering on the soft curve of her mouth. 'I've never wanted a woman as I want you,' he muttered. 'You're like an obsession with me. I wish to God I could understand why.'

'We always want what we can't have.'

'You think it's that simple, do you? You're wrong. Dead wrong . . . another tactic I was going to try was to play on your sympathies as far as Chris is concerned. Nothing fake about that, either. We've talked a lot the last couple of days, he and I—making up for lost time, I suppose. You'd be surprised how many times your name has cropped up. He really loves you, and if you and I were to marry, he, for one, would be delighted. It would make us a family, Meg.' Unconsciously his voice had deepened; he was leaning towards her, his very attitude one of urgency.

'A family in which one of the members isn't able to do most of the things the other two can? How long before that begins to pall? Before I became a nuisance, a hindrance?' She threw up her hands in passionate conviction. 'Don't you *see*? It wouldn't work! It couldn't work.'

His eyes met hers unflinchingly. 'I think it would.'

Her shoulders sagged. 'It wouldn't, Paul.'

He took a deep breath. Detaching her hands from the grass, where she was ruthlessly tearing the blades out by the roots, he held them in his, looking down at the slender fingers, at the tiny marks on her thumb where she had pricked herself with her needle. 'What if I told you I'd fallen in love with you? That everything else I've said today is only window dressing? That the real truth is that I love you, and that's why I want to marry you?'

Meg jerked her hands free, her voice ragged with pain. 'I'd say you're lying. That it's just another game with you, another way to make me do as you want.'

'Meg, are you even the slightest bit in love with me?'

There was a note in his voice she had never heard before—of pleading, or humility. 'No, Paul,' she answered very quietly, 'I'm sorry—but I'm not.'

'Then that's that, isn't it?' he said heavily. 'Let's go back.'

It took only twenty minutes for the return journey, although to Meg it seemed like forever. He hadn't meant what he had said about being in love with her—why, then, was she convinced that she had hurt him?

She had never been so glad to see the weatherbeaten shingles of the old fish shack. Punctiliously Paul took her to the door. 'Chris and I have to leave very early tomorrow morning to get to the airport for the first flight. So I'll say goodbye now.' He nodded curtly, turned on his heel, and strode up the slope.

Meg was visited by a wild urge to call him back, to tell him she'd changed her mind. Stuffing her fist to her mouth, she fought the words back. She was doing the right thing, the only thing . . . tears hanging on her lashes, she went inside and closed the door on the mocking brightness of the summer sun.

CHAPTER SEVEN

MEG never particularly liked the routine check-ups she had with the specialist in Halifax. She disliked being poked and prodded, unable to see the point of most of his questions. Besides, today she was completely out of sorts, for the drive in to the city with Ben had revived all the memories of her visits here with Paul and Chris, of the happy carefree days when they had been friends. However, she obediently tensed her leg muscles, wiggled her toes, and raised her knees as far as she could.

'Good,' the doctor said. 'Looks to me like you're ready. Sooner than I thought—interesting, that.'

His name was Dr Walter Moriarty. Meg had never really cared for him, sensing at their first meeting that she was not a person to him at all: simply a collection of nerves, bones, and muscles that didn't work as they should, a fact that seemed to both intrigue and annoy him, as if it were a personal affront. Now she said, 'Ready for what?'

'The operation, of course. Come now, Miss Cairns, you know I told you about it.'

Her mouth was dry. She said carefully, 'The first day I saw you, you mentioned once, very briefly, the possibility of an operation. You've never mentioned it since.'

He was plainly not convinced. 'Well, never mind that— I'm telling you now. You'll have to fly to Boston, the best man's there. He's a friend of mine—I'll give him a call right now and see what we can set up.'

He was about to leave the room, so she grabbed his white-coated arm. 'What will the operation *do*?'

He looked at her as if she were half-witted. 'There's a three to one chance it will make you walk again. Of course the converse is also true—there's the chance it could be unsuccessful. But you're young and healthy—a good risk, I'd say.' Fastidiously he removed her fingers from his sleeve. 'Now, if you'll pardon me, I'll place the call.'

Meg sat there on the examining table waiting for him to come back, her brain in a whirl, knowing that she would give almost anything to have Paul walk in the door. Paul, with his calmness and strength . . . but Paul was in Toronto and wouldn't be back for four or five days.

Dr Moriarty returned within five minutes, with what passed for a smile on his face. 'It's all arranged. My secretary's just checking that there's a seat on the flight tomorrow.'

'Tomorrow?' she repeated faintly.

'Yes—you're lucky. A cancellation in Thursday's operation schedule.' His phone rang and he picked up the receiver. 'Fine—that'll get her there in good time.' Addressing Meg again, he said, 'You can get the information from my secretary on the way out. And make an appointment to see me next month.' For a brief instant looking almost human, he added, 'Good luck, Miss Cairns.'

Meg was never really able to sort out clearly the events of the next few days. There were the explanations to Ben and Ada, and the hurriedly written notes to Paul and Chris. There was the flight to Boston and her arrival at the sprawling, ivy-covered brick hospital. Examinations, X-rays, blood tests, and then the operation, followed by the cautious days of appraisal through which she existed in a kind of a limbo. Then, miraculously, the first tentative steps in a metal walker, and the eventual move to crutches. The operation was a complete success, she was told; she would spend ten days in a rehabilitation clinic outside the city, and then fly home.

Noticing abstractedly that it was more important to phone Cairns Island first rather than phone Vancouver, and too excited to write, Meg dialled Ada's number. 'Ada? It's Meg. Ada, I can walk again—the operation worked!'

'Meg dear, that's wonderful news.' Had Meg not known Ada better, she would have said she was crying. 'Your grandfather's right here. I'll put him on.'

'I can walk, Grandpa!'

'Oh, lassie, that's the best piece of news I've ever had. When will you be home?'

Home . . . back to Cairns Island, to Ben and Ada, and of course to Paul and Chris. 'About a week and a half. Is Paul there?'

A slight pause. 'No, lass, they're not around just now. Listen, let me know your flight time and I'll meet you at the airport.'

Somehow she had had the vision of herself walking down the steps of the aircraft and straight into Paul's arms. 'That'll be lovely, Grandpa. I'll see you then. I'd better go, I don't have any more change. 'Bye.'

She hung up, feeling rather deflated; she had been counting on talking to Paul and Chris as well—that was one reason why she had phoned in the morning. She should have asked where they were, or left a number for Paul to phone back. Deciding she would leave getting in touch with her parents until the afternoon, she carefully walked back down the corridor to her room, aware of a deeper unease than that caused by Paul's absence this morning. Somehow she had expected a letter from him, some acknowledgement of the note she had left for him back at the island. But there had been nothing. No flowers, no letter or card. As her friend, surely he should have extended to her some kind of support throughout the ordeal of her operation and the days of uncertainty afterwards? Or had he, because of her continued refusal to marry him, simply cut her out of his life? But that left Chris—Chris would have sent her a picture he had coloured, or one of his laboriously printed messages, the letters straggling across the page . . . she was sure he would have.

She did not understand it . . . and in the privacy of her own room she could admit to herself how much this lack of communication was hurting her.

The ten days at the rehabilitation centre passed quickly. Although she still got very tired and often went back to a wheelchair in order to have a rest, she was nevertheless gaining far more confidence in her sense of balance and in the slowly increasing strength of her legs. Despite this, the doctor insisted she use a wheelchair for the return journey to Halifax; he gave her several typed sheets of instructions for her further progress and her exercises; and set up a schedule for her to use at home as far as physiotherapy and check-ups were concerned. And then she was on her way home . . .

She was the last person off the plane, one of the stewardesses wheeling her along the ramp to the baggage pick-up area. She saw Ben and Ada before they saw her— but there was no sign of Paul and Chris. Fixing a bright smile on her face, she called, 'Grandpa! Over here . . .'

He was looking unaccustomedly smart in a grey suit, his gold watch chain looped across the front. Ada, at his side, was wearing her best silk dress and her flowered hat that was reserved for ceremonial occasions only. In spite of Meg's crushing disappointment that neither Paul nor Chris was there to meet her, she was deeply touched to see Ada and Ben in all their finery. Before they could reach her, she asked the stewardess to stop the chair and stood up, carefully walking across the smooth-tiled floor to meet them.

There was no doubt about it this time—Ada *was* crying. Even Ben's eyes were suspiciously bright, and his voice was husky as he said, 'Welcome home, Meg,' hugging her with all his strength. Then they moved a little apart from each other and there was a sudden, awkward pause, which Ben rushed to fill. 'I'll get the chair for you—you mustn't get too tired. There's usually a five or ten-minute wait for the baggage.'

Ada pressed Meg's hand. 'It's grand seeing you on your feet, dear. We're so anxious to hear all the details. I'm sure you have to visit Dr Moriarty again soon, do you?'

Ben had brought the chair, and thankfully Meg subsided into it. 'Yes, I do, Ada.' Without a change of voice she went on, 'Where are Paul and Chris?'

Ada and Ben exchanged a quick glance of complicity. It was Ben who answered. 'Well now,' he said uncomfortably, 'we knew you'd be asking that. And you must have wondered why you haven't heard from them.'

Sheer terror suddenly swept over Meg, leaving her cold and shaking. Pressing her hands against the smooth wooden arms of the wheelchair, she said unevenly, 'They're all right, aren't they? Nothing's happened——'

'No, no, lass, it's nothing like that.' Ben patted her hand. 'Look, the baggage is starting to arrive. Let's go over and get it, and we'll explain on our way to the truck.'

Trying to keep her mind perfectly blank, Meg watched as Ben picked up her suitcase from the carousel. 'Just the one?' he asked.

'Yes, that's all.'

Then Ada was pushing her through the glass doors and out on to the concrete sidewalk. The sun was shining, although the air did not have the oppressive heat Meg had noticed in Boston. They went across the road to where the truck was parked; from the runway came the full-throated snarl of a jet-engine, which made conversation impossible. There was a further delay while Ben returned the wheelchair to the commissionaire. Then, finally, they were driving past the ranks of parked cars and the cluster of hangers to the four-lane highway.

Patiently Meg repeated, 'Where *are* Paul and Chris, Grandpa?'

He said bluntly, 'They've gone back to Toronto.'

'You mean—for good?'

'That's right.'

Feeling her way very carefully, she said, 'They went for Chris's check-up. Didn't they come back?'

'No, they didn't. Paul wrote to me a couple of days after they left. For one thing, apparently Chris's mother wanted to see Chris while they were there. Apart from that, Paul said he'd decided it would be better for Chris not to come back to the island, that he was getting too attached to it, and that he, Paul, thought they should both stay in the Toronto area for a while. He mentioned something about spending a couple of weeks at a friend's fishing lodge in northern Ontario.'

Because this was all too much to take in, Meg said, 'Chris's check-up . . . was he okay?'

'A hundred per cent.'

'That's good.'

'There are three letters for you at home,' Ben added. 'Two from Chris and one from Paul. I suppose we should have let you know earlier, lass, that they'd gone. But we were afraid it might harm your recovery, or worry you, so we decided to wait until you were home again.'

'I see.'

She was sitting by the window and now she stared fixedly at the passing scenery, the wide grass verges at the edge of the road and the monotonous stretch of forest. She felt hollow and bereft, and found her mind repeating the five little words over and over again, like a cracked record: Paul and Chris are gone ... Paul and Chris are gone. They would not be waiting at Ada's to see her walk across the grass. They would not be there to share in the joy of her recovery. They were gone. Gone, gone, gone ... Her throat tight with tension, she fought back the tears that threatened to flood her eyes. The trouble was that she knew, as Ben and Ada did not, the real reason why they were gone. It was because she had refused to marry Paul and thereby provide a mother for Chris. Paul wasn't worried about Chris's attachment to the island; he was worried about Chris's attachment to her. He had removed Chris from her presence, presumably believing that the boy would soon forget her, and that the few brief weeks on the island would fade into a distant memory, an interlude unrelated to the daily business of living.

Only now that she knew it had become impossible did she realise how strongly she had been counting on seeing Paul again. She was no longer tied to a wheelchair ... she could walk again, and in time would learn to run and jump and dance, to scramble over rocks and stand on the deck of a rolling boat. The operation had removed the impediment to their marriage, so that what remained was the fun and laughter of their friendship, the conversation that had ranged over every possible subject, the sexual awareness that had flared between them at the slightest touch, the liking that maybe, just maybe, could have deepened and matured into love.

But Paul, knowing nothing of her operation, had gone, and her half-formulated hopes lay about her in ruins.

It was an effort to bring herself back to the present, but she suddenly realised she had been quiet for far too long. 'Sorry,' she said lightly. 'I've been daydreaming. Remind me when we get home to call Dr Moriarty's office—I'm supposed to go and see him this week.'

'Tell us about your stay—did they look after you well?' Ada asked, and Meg launched into a description of the past few weeks, even managing to make amusing stories out of several little incidents. Then Ben told her about the ups and downs of the lobster and mackerel fishing, and Ada related the latest doings of her assorted children and grandchildren. Before Meg knew it, they were driving down the winding road to the cove and parking by the bridge.

'You look tired, lass—I'll get your wheelchair. You mustn't overdo it,' Ben said firmly.

'He's going to fuss over you like a mother hen,' Ada said indulgently as Ben strode across the bridge. 'He cried like a baby when he heard the operation had been successful.'

Out of the blue Meg heard herself ask, 'Why don't you marry Ben, Ada?'

Ada blinked, shifting in her seat. 'We're comfortable as we are,' she replied, a faint note of defensiveness in her voice.

'You're obviously very fond of him,' Meg persisted.

'Indeed I am.'

'He seems so lonely sometimes—no wife, his only son on the opposite side of the country . . .'

With something of her normal acerbity Ada said, 'He's well rid of both of them. Harriet was never a good wife to him, she was always trying to get him to move to the city and take what she called a more respectable job—can you imagine Ben behind a desk all day? As for your father, he was just like her—looked down his nose at Ben and

Cairns Island as if they weren't good enough for him. That's why I'm so glad you've come, dearie—you've given Ben a lot of happiness this summer.'

'I love him and the island,' Meg said simply. 'But it's not just a granddaughter he needs, Ada—it's a wife.'

'Well now, if we did get married, which house would we live in? He wouldn't want to close up his, and I wouldn't want to leave mine. And what on earth would my children think of me getting married at my age?'

'Those are just excuses, and well you know it.'

Ada pleated the flowered silk folds of her dress. 'Yes, well, there's my Jonathan, you see . . . gone these ten years and still I miss him. I'm afraid if I married Ben it wouldn't be the same.'

Ben was coming back across the bridge, pushing the chair in front of him. 'You couldn't expect it to be the same,' Meg said urgently. 'Ben and Jonathan are two different people. But it could be very rewarding——' She had to break off, because Ben had arrived.

Ada had prepared a delicious dinner, and it was mid-evening when Meg finally said, 'I must get to bed—I'm tired out. Thank you both for coming to the airport, and thanks for the lovely meal, Ada.'

'You're welcome. You *do* look tired. You'll be all right now, will you?' Ada hesitated before bringing up a subject they had avoided all evening. 'You were upset about Paul and Chris, I know.'

'Yes, I was.'

'So indeed was I. I thought they were both happy here—you could have knocked me over with a feather when I got Paul's letter. Ah well, surely they'll be back for a visit—perhaps he'll say something about it in your letter.'

The letters . . . Meg felt her stomach cramp with ap-prehension. She took her chair down to the little shack and went indoors, turning on the lights. Ada had been busy while she was away, for the place was spotlessly clean, a pleasant trace of lemon oil lingering in the air. A bowl of garden flowers had been placed in the centre of the table, while propped up against it were the three white envelopes, together with the notes she, Meg, had left for Paul and Chris, which they had never seen.

Trying to avoid looking at them, she moved slowly around the room, unpacking a few things and getting ready for bed. She felt very tired, both from the day's long journey and from all the emotional strain, and it was a temptation to leave the letters until the next day. But when she finally got into bed, she had the letters in her hand. She opened Paul's first. It was dated two days after he had gone to Toronto; there was no return address. She had not seen his handwriting before; it was angular and forceful, very much what she would have expected. Her eyes ran down the closely written page.

Dear Meg,

It seems obvious you have no intention of marrying me, now or in the future. Therefore I have decided that Chris and I should leave Cairns Island, because he is far too fond of you already. I hope he'll get over that and settle down with me in the Toronto area. The doctors assure me he has made a phenomenal recovery from the operation, and for your part in that, I thank you. Although I don't imagine I'll be seeing you again, Meg, I'll always remember you.

Paul.

No return address, no prospect of a visit. A very final letter, the severing of a relationship. Hot tears were making the ink run on the page, and furiously Meg scrubbed at her eyes. She hadn't expected anything different, had she? So why was she crying?

Paul had obviously had a hand in Chris's two letters, for he had printed an address at the top of each of them, care of Mrs Oliver Whitely . . . Annette, Chris's mother. Was Paul *that* determined that she not have his own address? Or had he, as he had mentioned earlier, sold his house and therefore was without an address? Chris himself had printed the letters. Smudged and erased as they were, the message was clear. The first said, 'I miss you,' and the second, 'Please write.' Each was signed, 'Love, Chris.'

She was crying too hard to stop now. The letters fell to the floor as she turned off the light and buried her face in the pillows. Paul and Chris had gone from her life, and would not be back . . .

CHAPTER EIGHT

A WEEK went by. To an outside observer it would have appeared to be a busy, productive week for Meg. She had an appointment with Dr Moriarty, who condescended to approve the work of his Boston colleague; and on the same day she saw the physiotherapist, who set up a programme of exercises which she did religiously every day. Kevin came for a visit, his happiness at her recovery so genuine and heartfelt that she was touched. Morning and afternoon she went for a walk, either alone or accompanied by Ben. She worked on her embroidery. She lay out on the grass in her shorts and halter top until her skin was tanned an even gold. And all the time three-quarters of her mind was preoccupied with the two people who were absent, those with whom, most of any in the world, she had wanted to share her recovery: Paul and Chris.

Everywhere she turned on the island there were memories of them, to the point where it did not seem possible they were gone. She would climb the slope to Ada's expecting to see Chris trotting along beside Ben, or to hear the staccato notes of Paul's typewriter. Whenever someone knocked at her door, she had to quell the crazy hope that it was Paul coming to invite her out or Chris arriving to flop down on the floor and colour or read.

On her daily walks she had deliberately avoided taking the path that led to the beach and the lighthouse. But finally late one hot afternoon when she had been home for over a week she found herself walking along the trail, her feet cushioned by the soft grass. The air smelled of wild roses and spruce resin, overlaid with the crispness of the sea. The tide was out, the sand blindingly bright in the sun. Meg climbed down the path where Paul had carried her and sat down with her back against the same rock. The first time he had kissed her had been here . . .

Sharp as a knife, her longing for him pierced her. She would have given almost anything to see his tall, broad-shouldered figure coming towards her, to hear the laughter that had so often warmed his deep voice, to watch him smile at her, his dark eyes intent on her face . . . Nor would that be enough. She wanted him to kiss her again and again until the demands of his mouth brought her whole body to life. She wanted to feel his hands on her, strong and sure, to touch him and be held by him. She wanted to love and be loved by him . . .

Her shocked blue eyes gazed at the far shore. She loved Paul Moreton, she thought dazedly. That was why she couldn't get him out of her mind, and why she longed for his physical presence until her whole body ached with it. She had been deceiving herself that all she felt for him was liking and friendship; she felt that, certainly, but there was more: that intangible, impossible-to-define emotion called love, that had, she realised in something akin to panic, without her even knowing it bound her to Paul with ties from which she might never escape. He was the only man she had ever met who could bring her alive sexually; the only man with whom she could share all the thoughts that came into her head. Her laughter and joy, her anger and frustration and tears—he had seen and accepted them all, for he had the inner strength and integrity that could allow her to be fully herself.

This was the man she had three times refused to marry. The reasons at the time had been the right ones, she was still convinced of that. But the reasons no longer existed. She could walk now. She was no longer confined to a wheelchair, so often dependent on other people. And by one of those cruel ironies of fate Paul had removed himself from her life before he could know of her altered circumstances.

She got up, unable to stand the tenor of her thoughts. Without conscious volition her feet carried her farther down the path to the lighthouse, to the rock where they had sat so close together and where Paul had for the last time tried to break down her resistance to marrying him. 'What if I told you I'd fallen in love with you?' he had

said. Was there the slightest chance he had meant it? Or
had it simply been another tactic he had used to persuade
her to fall in with his wishes? She would never know
now . . .

Driven by a restlessness too insistent to be ignored, she
walked back to the shack far more quickly than she had
walked out. Even then she could not settle down quietly
to her needlework, so she went across the bridge and
explored a couple of the little side tracks that meandered
from the road through the scrub and the tumbled rocks.
One of them led to yet another inlet of the sea where she
startled a heron; it rose ponderously into the sky on its
massive grey and white wings. The other trail wound its
way farther and farther across the barrens, where every
rock and shrub looked the same. If it was this confusing
in daylight, she could understand all too easily how Chris
had got lost after dark. By now her legs were starting to
tremble from over-exertion, so she sat on a boulder to
rest, gazing out over the primitive grandeur of the landscape, a study of greys and greens and the related blues
of sea and sky. Harsh, bleak, barren—those adjectives
would certainly apply. Yet it was also beautiful in its stark
simplicity and lack of compromise. It was a landscape,
she thought whimsically as she stood up to leave, in which
Paul Moreton would be quite at home and Philip totally
out of place.

By the time she reached the shack the sun was providing
a dazzling display of pink and orange and yellow at the
horizon and the air was considerably cooler. Knowing she
had walked much too far for one day, she subsided into
her wheelchair and rested for a while before making a
simple meal out of cold meats and a salad. Clearing away
the dishes, she changed into her long blue robe, knowing
it would not be long before she was in bed; she was so
tired that her mind had succeeded in blanking out the
continual pain of Paul's absence, so exacerbated today by
the discovery that she loved him. She picked out a book
from the collection on the shelves and wheeled herself over
by the lamp to read, soothed by the rhythmic advance
and retreat of the waves on the rocks. Within half an

hour her eyelids were beginning to droop.

The knock on the door was so unexpected that for a moment she wondered if she had imagined it. The book open in her lap, she waited to see if it would be repeated. The second time it was sharper, more impatient. There was only one person she knew who would knock like that. The colour drained from her face and when she called, 'Come in,' her voice was thin.

The man who entered was the man whom earlier she would have given anything to see; it was as if her wishes had conjured him up. She said faintly, 'Hello, Paul.'

He stepped inside, closing the door carefully behind him. He seemed bigger than she remembered. The lamp-light threw his shadow on the wall behind him, dark and distorted. Then he stepped forward into the light and she saw the lines of strain around his mouth and the hard-set features. 'Where's Chris?' she said, suddenly afraid.

'He's in Bayfield. At the bed and breakfast place we were looking for the night we met you. It seemed— appropriate to stay there.' His voice was heavy with irony.

'Why are you here?' she whispered.

'That's a long story. May I sit down?'

'Of course.'

He pulled up the chair he had so often sat on before and she had to clasp the covers of the book to remind herself that this was real . . . that Paul, who had scarcely left her thoughts all day, was actually sitting only a couple of feet away from her. He had been scrutinising her, and now he said, 'You look tired. And you've lost weight.'

'Oh.' Meg searched her brain for something a little more intelligent than that. 'I thought you were in Toronto.'

'I was.' His mouth thinned. 'And I'd planned to stay there.'

There was no mistaking the anger in his voice. 'So why are you here?' she asked, holding even more tightly to the book so he would not guess that her hands were shaking.

'Because of Chris—and believe me, it's only because of Chris. If it hadn't been for him, I wouldn't have come within a hundred miles of this place again.'

'What's Chris done?' she asked.

'What hasn't he done would be more like it. We went up to Toronto and he had his check-up and that was fine. Then we went to a friend's fishing lodge for a few days— Chris wasn't very keen, he wanted to come straight back here—to you; but I managed to persuade him he'd have fun at the camp. I, you see, had already decided neither of us was coming back here, for the reasons I stated in my letter. I broke this news to him after we'd been at the camp for a week. He didn't believe me at first, thought I was joking. Then he threw a temper tantrum and eventually cried himself to sleep. The next day he stowed away on the jeep that was going back to Kapuskasing for supplies, with the idea, so he told me later after I'd caught up with him, of phoning his mother to get her to send him back to Nova Scotia. You've got to give the kid credit for brains—and persistence.'

Meg closed her eyes briefly. This was worse than anything she could have anticipated. 'What did he do next?' she asked fatalistically.

'Wrote you a letter, saying he missed you. He was okay for a few days because he was so sure you'd write right back. You didn't even bother to answer it, did you, Meg? Or the next one. But even that didn't stop him from wanting to see you again. I tried everything I could to distract him—took him swimming, tenting, to the zoo, to the movies. He went along with me and I think he even tried to enjoy himself, and every day he got a little more listless, a little more apathetic. He started losing weight, then he got the 'flu and spent a week in bed. It nearly broke my heart, because he was beginning to look like the boy I found when I got back from Africa, and I couldn't stand that. So one day I asked him what he'd like to do that day if he had his choice.'

Paul got up from the chair, pacing restlessly around the room. 'You can guess what he said. He'd like to see Meg, he said. And I knew I was beaten.'

She licked her lips. 'Why didn't you bring him with you tonight?'

'Because it was late when we got to Bayfield and he's

still feeling some of the after-effects of 'flu. So I packed him off to bed with the firm promise he could come to-morrow; the lady who runs the place has a teenaged niece — who's babysitting.'

His eyes were on her face. She had always thought they were expressive eyes; she had never seen them so cold, so inscrutable. She had to say something, anything, to break the silence. 'I'm sorry you've had so much trouble.'

'Are you, Meg? Are you really sorry?'

She held on to her temper. 'Perhaps I should have said I'm sorry Chris has been unhappy.'

'I'm going to give you the chance to show you're sincere.'

'I do wish you'd stop prowling around like a—a caged lion,' she said, with spirit if no particular originality.

'It's about the only way I can keep my hands off you.'

Refusing to be itimidated, she snapped, 'Will you tell me what I'm supposed to have done?'

'Wound your way around that boy's heart so he's lost without you—that's all,' Paul said sarcastically.

'That's hardly my fault!'

He glared at her. 'Believe it or not, I didn't come here to yell at you. And you're quite right—it really isn't your fault.' Thrusting his hands in the pockets of his whipcord trousers, he leaned against the table, crossing his long legs.

Sensing that he was genuinely trying to control himself, Meg said more quietly, 'Why did you come?'

A lock of dark hair had fallen across his forehead. He pushed it back irritably and said with a coldness that hurt Meg more than his anger, 'Not to ask you to marry me, you can be sure of that—I'm not going to make more of a fool of myself than I already have. I want to employ you, Meg—as a companion for Chris. I'll pay you a salary, give you regular days off, sick leave, the works. In return for that I want you to spend as much time with him through the day as possible. For now we'll have to live on the island. But I'm going to make an offer on a house at Harrington Beach and I hope the deal will go through quickly and we can move out there.'

'You mean you want me to *live* with you?'

'Don't worry—I'll get a live-in housekeeper to look after the proprieties. And there'll be no emotional entanglements, Meg. This will be strictly a business arrangement.'

If it hadn't been so awful, it might almost have been funny, it was such a travesty of all her hopes. One thing was sure: she had the answer to her question. Paul Moreton did not love her. Hate her, maybe. But love her, no.

'I want you to think it over until tomorrow,' he went on stiffly. 'I'll bring Chris over—oh, probably after lunch. You can give me your answer then.'

'What if I say no?'

He straightened slowly. 'I have no idea what I'll do if you refuse. You might keep in mind that the salary will be more than adequate, and will certainly give you your much-vaunted independence.'

Did he think she was only motivated by money? 'I'll be sure to keep that in mind,' she said sarcastically.

'Good. Until tomorrow then, Meg. I'll let myself out. Goodnight.' One last inimical look before he turned away and walked across the room.

The latch clicked shut behind him. For a few moments Meg sat in frozen stillness, then on a sudden impulse she wheeled across the room, locked the door, and drew the curtains across the window by the sink.

It was the cold smoothness of the metal rims of her chair that brought her to a sudden horrified realization of what she had failed to do. She had been so shocked by Paul's sudden appearance, so mesmerised by his anger and his coldness, that she had not told him about her operation; she had been sitting in her wheelchair as if nothing had changed. So he did not know that she could walk . . . how could she have been so stupid, so stunned?

And what would he say when he did find out? Would he ask her to marry him again? Somehow, remembering his hostility this evening, it did not seem very likely.

Because her thoughts kept churning around and around in her head that night, she slept poorly, and in the morn-

ing looked pale and heavy-eyed. A hot shower improved
her outlook on life, and she brushed her hair dry outdoors
in the sun. It was going to be impossible to work this
morning, she knew that, so maybe she'd go over to Kevin's
shop and take him the articles she'd already completed—
it would give her something to do, and pass the time until
Paul and Chris arrived. Just then Ben came out of his
back door on his way to the toolshed. She called to him
and he ambled across the grass towards her. 'Morning,
Meg. Going to be a grand day. Although the wind'll likely
change by evening.'

She patted the grass beside her. 'Sit down a minute—
I've got some news for you.'

He squatted on his heels, taking out his pipe and beginning to fill it with the strongly smelling tobacco that
he favoured. 'What's up?'

'Paul's back.'

She noticed that he did not look particularly surprised.
'Is he now?' he said slowly.

'Don't tell me you were expecting him?'

'I kind of thought he might be back. Is Chris with
him?'

'Yes. They're both coming here after lunch. Paul wants
me to work for him, Grandpa. A paid companion for
Chris.' She could not completely keep the hurt from her
voice.

'Well now, that might not be a bad idea. Give you the
chance to look around a bit and get your bearings—see
what you want to do with your life now that you can
walk again. And you're fond of the boy—that's no problem.'

And far too fond of his father, she could have said.
'You think I should do it?'

He struck a match, cupping his hands around the bowl
of his pipe as he lit the tobacco. Clouds of blue smoke
wafted around his face. 'Sure I do.' He grinned at her.
'In the meantime I'm going over to Camden to pick up a
few things—want to come?'

'I was going to ask you if you were going. I want to
take some things to Kevin.'

'Ready in ten minutes?'.

'Sure.'

They both got to their feet, and briefly Ben rested his gnarled fingers in her shoulder. 'Lassie, it's like a miracle every time you do that.'

Meg smiled at him in perfect understanding. It *was* a miracle . . . and one she would be able to share with Paul this afternoon. She drew in a deep breath of the morning air, feeling herself come tinglingly alive. She was going to see Paul again—and he had placed in her hands the opportunity to see more and more of him and his son. All her doubts disappeared and she knew with crystal clearness that she was going to accept Paul's offer. 'I'll go and get changed,' she said, favouring Ben with a brilliant smile. 'I'll be ready in five minutes.'

She wanted a change from her usual clothes. In the back of her closet she found a slim-fitting dress of leaf-green cotton that she had not worn since the accident; the skirt was slit up the sides, revealing rather more of her slender, tanned legs than was usually visible. A matching eye-shadow. Mascara to darken her lashes. Gold hoops in her ears. She looked at herself in the mirror with justifiable satisfaction before gathering up the neat pile of finished work to take to Kevin.

His shop was on the ground floor of a wood-framed house that was nearly two hundred years old, the home of generations of sea captains; it was built on a knoll on the outskirts of town overlooking the ocean, its hand-carved eaves and door posts painted white, the shingles a sturdy rust-red. Kevin had filled the flowerbeds with asters and stocks and Sweet Williams and the lawn was a smooth vivid green.

Her grandfather dropped her off and went to do his errands, and she walked up the flagstone path, pleased to see that there were a number of cars in the parking lot.

A bell tinkled as she pushed open the door. She had not been inside for some weeks and she paused to admire Kevin's artfully arranged display of paintings, hand-stitched quilts, pewter, jewellery, and handcrafts, her own embroidery included. He was talking to a couple of customers, so she wandered around happily, inspecting some of the work more closely. It was ten minutes before he came over to her. 'Hey, you look great!' he said.

'Thank you! I brought you a couple of sets of place mats and some guest towels, as well as the crewel-work pictures.'

'I'll give you a receipt. And let me introduce you to these ladies—they were hoping to see more of your work.'

It was while she was chatting to the women, who were tourists from New England, that she noticed through the square-paned windows that Ben's truck had drawn up outside. 'I'm afraid you'll have to excuse me—my grandfather is waiting for me,' she murmured.

She was at the door when Kevin called, 'Hold it, Meg! Your receipt.' They went outside together, Kevin checking his addition as he went. 'I've got it right—thanks, Meg.' He smiled at her, his blunt-featured face without guile. 'It's fantastic to see you out and about like this.' He hugged her hard and she felt the roughness of his beard against her skin as he kissed her on the cheek. 'Look after yourself.'

'I will.'

He went back into the shop and she began walking down the path, her eyes on the ground, because some of the stones were uneven, the sea breeze tossing her blonde hair and moulding her dress to her body. She never knew what it was that made her look up. A car had parked ahead of Ben's truck, and a tall, dark-haired man was standing beside it, staring up at her. Her heart skipped a beat and she stumbled slightly. She stood still, fighting back an actual wave of dizziness as Paul started up the path towards her, his movements with none of their usual loose-limbed grace. He was walking like a man in shock. As he got closer she saw his face was dead white, his eyes blank, almost unfocussed.

He stopped within a foot of her. As though feeling his way through a world that had suddenly turned upside down, he said hoarsely, 'You can walk.'

'Yes. I had an operation a week after——'

He cut across her, his voice anguished. 'Why didn't you tell me last night?'

'I——'

'You were in your wheelchair. I didn't even suspect—why in God's name didn't you *tell* me?'

Meg swallowed hard. 'Until last night I didn't think I was ever going to see you again. And then you walked in the door as if you'd never been away and started telling me about Chris and asking me to work for you . . .' She faltered to a stop. 'And . . . and then you were gone before I could even catch my breath. It sounds ridiculous, I suppose, but I honestly didn't even think about telling you until after you'd left.'

'Dear God,' Paul said heavily, passing a hand over his face, 'this changes everything.'

'It doesn't have to,' she said sharply.

It was doubtful if he heard her. 'And I haven't even told you how glad I am for you.' His hand dropped on her shoulder, but before he could say anything else there came the slam of a car door and Chris came hurtling up the path. Paul broke his headlong rush. 'Easy, now—don't go knocking Meg over!'

'Ben told me you could walk again!' Chris shrilled, jumping up and down in excitement despite Paul's restraining hand. 'Can you run yet?'

'Not yet—but I should be able to fairly soon.'

'Can you go swimming?'

'Yes, I'm allowed to do that. Although I haven't so far.'

'Dad, let's go to the beach this afternoon—we could take Meg swimming!'

'We have to go and see Ada——'

'We could do that now. Please, Dad?'

Paul turned to the girl. 'Meg?'

With the sense that she was deciding on something far more significant than an afternoon at the beach, Meg said, 'That would be fun.'

'Yippee!' Chris yelled. 'Let's go see Ada right now, Dad.'

'Okay, okay, take it easy.' Crooking his elbow, Paul suggested, 'Take my arm, Meg.'

She tucked her hand into his elbow, her fingers touching the bare skin of his forearm, for his sleeves were rolled up. Chris ran round to the other side, grabbing her hand. Happiness winged through her, and she said spontaneously, 'I'm so glad you're both back—I missed you!'

'I missed you, too,' said Chris, dragging at her arm. Then, accusingly, 'You didn't answer my letters.'

She looked down at him. 'I didn't get them until last week, Chris—I was in Boston for about a month, you see, and all that time your letters were at Cairns Island. That's why I didn't write to you.'

He digested this in silence, then said with a peculiarly adult air of wisdom, '*That's* all right, then.'

If only matters between her and Paul could be dealt with as easily, she thought ruefully, as Paul helped her up into the truck; he had not, she noticed, suggested that she ride back with them. Ben turned the truck around and they started for home. 'Ada'll be glad to see them,' he remarked. 'Be good for her to have the little fellow around again. She's been a bit down the last couple of days.'

'Oh? What do you mean?'

'Well, she's picked up a cold, for one thing. Come to think of it, it might be better if Chris stayed at my place until it's cleared up. But apart from that, she's been kind of low in her mind.' He sighed. 'Mind you, it was this time of year when Jonathan got drowned—maybe that's what it is.'

Meg patted his knee. 'Let's hope Paul and Chris will cheer her up, then,' she said, her heart aching for Ben, whose patient, undemanding love for Ada seemed doomed to go unrewarded.

When they got back to Cairns Island, Meg went straight home. She hunted out her bikini and put it on under a matching flowered sundress, then brushed her hair back into a ponytail. This afternoon she must make it clear to Paul, she thought, that she would accept his offer of a job. After last night she was more than ever convinced he did not love her, and she winced away from the thought that he might repeat his offer of marriage, for she did not think she could bear him to do that, loving him as she did and knowing herself unloved; equally she knew she could not bear it if again he and his son disappeared from her life. To take his offered position as Chris's companion was a solution of kinds, the only one available.

Meg was gathering up her towel and a sunhat when she heard the rush of steps across the ramp. 'Hi, Chris!' she called.

'Dad's ready—are you?'

They walked up the slope and over the bridge to where Paul was waiting in the car. Chris slid in the middle and Meg got in behind him, and they set off, Paul keeping the conversation to commonplaces by intention, the girl was sure, rather than by accident. The beach was on the next peninsula to the west; because it was a considerable distance from any towns, there were only a few cars parked along the track that led behind the dunes. Paul drove nearly to the end of the road before parking the car. 'I loathe crowded beaches,' he said lazily. 'Get your stuff out of the back, Chris, and don't go in the water until we get there.'

Predictably Chris had disappeared over the top of the dunes before Meg and Paul had even left the car. Carrying assorted towels and a beach basket, they followed him across the sand. Purple-flowering beach pea was entangled with the sharp-edged grasses; the sand shifted under their feet as they walked, and at the crest of the dunes Meg stopped for a brief rest. The beach was a long sickle-shaped curve, ending to her right in a small promontory of rocks topped by wind-bent spruce trees, while at its far end were clustered the half dozen or so houses of the village. The breakers rushed in to shore in serried white ranks, dotted here and there with swimmers. Chris, already stripped down to his swimsuit, his red bucket and shovel in his hand, was standing at the very edge of the water.

As Meg kicked off her sandals, Paul spread out the car rug on the sand in a hollow sheltered from the breeze. He dropped his shirt on the rug, following it with his jeans, and straightened to his full height, wearing only close-fitting blue swim trunks. His body was evenly tanned, from the deep chest narrowing to his waist, to the long, muscular legs. Once again she noticed the two parallel scars on his back, ugly reminders of his sojourn in a foreign prison.

She fiddled with the belt of her wrap-around dress, knowing she should remove it, yet shy to do so. Paul grinned at her unsympathetically, and she knew he was aware of her dilemma. 'Hurry up,' he said. 'Chris is waiting.'

She slid her arms out of the dress and laid it on the rug, her cheeks tinged with colour. There were only a couple of feet between them, not nearly enough for her peace of mind, and she said breathlessly, 'I hadn't realised how much taller than me you are,' taking an involuntary step backwards as she spoke; her head only reached to his chin.

In one swift glance he encompassed her figure: the firm high breasts; curving waist and hips; long, slender legs. 'You're so very beautiful,' he said softly. 'But then I'm sure you've been told that many times before.'

She had . . . but it had never touched her as it did now. 'I like it when you tell me.'

He reached out and cupped her shoulders in his palms, gently rubbing the sun-warmed flesh. 'I can't tell you how happy I am for you, Meg—to see you walking is like a miracle.' His kiss was simply an extension of his words; she swayed towards him, her eyes shut, and for a few brief seconds they stood body to body, his hands sliding down her back to hold her by the hips, her palms resting on the dark mat of hair on his chest.

Not ten feet away a small voice piped, 'Why are you kissing Meg, Dad?' Then, hopefully, 'Are you going to marry her?'

Abruptly Meg was freed. For the first time since she had met him she saw Paul momentarily at a loss for words, and knew she had been given her chance. 'No, Chris,' she said lightly, 'we're not getting married. Your father was kissing me because he's happy that I'm able to walk again. But I *am* going to be staying with you the whole summer and probably even longer, because I'm going to be working for your father and my job will be to look after you.' She hesitated. 'Will you like that?'

The boy looked from one to the other of them. 'We won't be going back to Toronto, though?'

Paul answered. 'No, Chris. I told you we'd buy a house around here somewhere.'

'And Meg would come and live with us?'

'That's right.'

'Okay!' Chris grinned at Meg, showing all the gaps in his teeth. 'I'm making a sand castle—want to help?'

'Of course.'

But before she could follow the boy's darting figure down the beach to the water's edge, Paul said silkily, 'Smoothly done, Miss Cairns.' Her eyes widened questioningly. 'Don't look so innocent—you know perfectly well what you've done. Accepted the job, turned down the marriage—and both in such a way that I couldn't say a word.'

'You did offer me the job,' she said defensively.

'So I did—before I knew about your operation. Since then, of course, I might have thought the better of it.' She opened her mouth to speak, but he forestalled her. His eyes were brimming with anger even though his voice remained level. 'Don't worry, I get the rest of the message—the part you didn't say. That you don't want to marry me in any circumstances. In that respect, your operation didn't really change anything, did it? What excuse are you going to give me now?

'How about that you don't love me?' she said boldly.

His eyelids flickered. 'I see. In the interests of honesty, let's also add that you don't love me.'

She did, she did . . . perhaps never more so than now, when his big, nearly naked body towered over her and his words beat against her like flails. She turned away abruptly, afraid that he would see the truth written in her eyes. 'I'm going to help Chris.'

'That's right—because that's your job, isn't it?' Paul snarled.

She was goaded into replying. 'It's what you wanted

ever since we met, isn't it? So why are you complaining now that you've got it?'

'If you don't know, Meg, far be it for me to tell you.'

'You're impossible!' She stamped her foot in the sand, then winced as the pain shot up her leg.

'Are you all right?' The anger was gone from his voice, leaving nothing but concern.

'Mmm . . . I shouldn't have done that—silly of me.'

He held out his hand. 'Let's call a truce and go and help Chris with his sand castle.' She signified her agreement by placing her hand in his, a little reluctantly, and together they walked down to the sea. But their argument had taken the shine from the day for Meg, for even though they played with Chris and swam and picnicked, and even though it was a kind of celebration of her new freedom, she could not deceive herself that she and Paul were nearly as close as they had been in those earlier, golden days when they had called each other friends. Nor did the next couple of days mitigate that impression; in fact, it seemed as though Paul was purposely leaving her and Chris alone together, removing himself either to work on his book, or to travel around the countryside with the real estate agent. Meg tried not to let this hurt her, but, of course, inevitably it did. In a subtle way she could not have put her finger on, she had changed from Paul's friend to his employee and it was obvious he meant to leave her alone to get on with her job.

CHAPTER NINE

Dr Moriarty had advised Meg against driving a car for a while, so of necessity she and Chris spent much of their time on the island—not that either of them minded that very much. Because Ada had developed a severe bronchial cough, Meg was particularly glad to stay close to home, helping Ada whenever possible with housework and meals.

Meg and Chris were coming back from the little beach at Flat Rock one day and met Paul just leaving Ada's; he was wearing a pair of faded denim shorts and nothing else, and as always Meg felt her heart constrict with love for him. He grinned at them, stretching lazily. 'I've been working too hard,' he complained. 'What have you two been up to?'

Chris held out his bucket. 'I caught a crab. He's hiding in the seaweed, see? Do you think Ada will let me keep him in the house?'

'I should think it's highly unlikely,' his father replied, peering into the bucket. 'Especially as she's not feeling very well. Why don't you put him in one of the tide pools down by the bridge? If you leave him in the bucket, he'll die.'

'That's what Meg said, too,' Chris replied in disgust, obviously reluctant to give up his prize.

'I could come down with you,' Paul suggested. 'If we find a fairly large pool, you might be able to catch him again tomorrow.'

Chris seemed to accept this idea. 'Let's go right now,' he said. 'Oh, look, Dad—there's a man coming.'

A very large black car had parked beside Ben's truck, and a man was walking across the bridge. Paul said without much interest, 'We'll have to give him directions, Chris—he's probably lost. He doesn't look like the type to come here on purpose.' The man was closer now and walking up the grass verge; he was wearing exquisitely pressed white flannels and spotless white shoes, with a white shirt, a silk ascot, and a navy blue blazer, a crest on its breast pocket. He was tall and slim, his dark hair neatly slicked down from a side parting. Mirrored dark glasses hid his eyes.

Paul called out hospitably, 'Can I help you? Lost your way?'

Meg made a strangled noise in her throat but no one paid her any attention. The stranger called back, 'No, I believe I have the right place—Cairns Island? In fact, there you are, Margaret.'

Paul's head swung round. 'You know him?'

'Yes,' she stuttered. 'Yes, I do. It's Philip ... you remember I told you about him ...'

Philip quickly covered the last few yards. Going straight up to Meg, he put his arms around her and kissed her as if he had every right to do so. 'Hello, darling. Marvellous to see you again.' Standing back a little, his hands still on her shoulders, he looked her up and down, from her untidy, sun-bleached hair to her bare feet; she was wearing brief shorts and a bikini top, her tanned face innocent of make-up. 'I wasn't sure it was you at first—but you look wonderfully well.'

It was her turn to say something. Finding her tongue, she said, 'Hello, Philip—this is quite a surprise. You've come a long way.'

He flicked her cheek with his finger. 'And all just to see you—you should be flattered.'

She was not at all sure of her feelings, but she did not think flattered was a particularly accurate description of them. Trying to maintain a semblance of normality, she said, 'Philip, let me introduce my friends, Paul Moreton and his son Chris. This is Philip Saunders, Paul a—a friend from Vancouver.'

'I do remember you telling me about him,' said Paul, an edge to his voice. 'How do you do?' The two men shook hands warily, and then Chris, transferring his bucket to the other hand, insisted on shaking hands too, no doubt transferring a fair bit of sand from his hand to Philip's in the process.

Philip had taken off his glasses. His eyes were his least attractive feature, being a very pale grey; apart from that he was an outstandingly handsome man, his features having an almost classical perfection. Without appearing to do so, he must have taken in Paul's costume—or rather, lack of it—and now said with the faintest hint of patronage, 'You must be one of the local people, Mr Moreton?'

'By no means,' Paul said smoothly. 'Chris and I are summer visitors from Toronto.'

'Paul is a well-known journalist,' Meg said shortly.

'Moreton . . . not the Moreton who's done so much reporting from the newly developing African countries?'

Paul nodded. 'That's me,' he said ungrammatically.

'I'd heard you were in prison over there.'

'I was. I got out,' was the economical reply.

Philip frowned slightly, plainly reassessing his first impression of Paul and not particularly liking what he had found out. 'Are you staying nearby?'

'In the white house.' Casually Paul indicated Ada's pristinely painted home.

'I see.'

Meg had had enough of this verbal fencing. 'How are my mother and father, Philip? Have you seen them lately?'

'As a matter of fact, I'm here as your father's emissary. He was rather too busy to come himself.'

'Naturally,' she said ironically. 'He always is.'

'I don't think you quite understand the demands of his work, Margaret. He's been under a lot of pressure lately. He's taken on the presidency of a new company, as well, so that's added to the burden.'

As long as she had known him, Philip had always been on her father's side. Giving him a bright, false smile, she said lightly, 'And why are you here as his emissary, Philip?'

He glanced over at the others. 'Perhaps we could go somewhere where we could talk more privately, Margaret?'

Paul said drily, 'We were about to leave anyway. Nice to meet you, Philip, and we'll see you later, Meg. Come on, Chris, let's take the crab down to the shore.'

Hand in hand the two of them turned away, and Meg fought back a sensation of being deserted. Once they were out of earshot, she said to Philip, 'What's the real reason you've come, Philip?'

He looked around him, apparently oblivious to the sparkling beauty of the calm blue waters of the cove. 'Is there somewhere we can go to talk? Are you living in the other house?' He indicated Ben's.

'No,' she said mischievously, pointing out the weathered little building on stilts out over the rocks. 'I live in the fish shack.'

'Good God, you live in *that*?'

Knowing exactly what he was thinking, she said, 'It's a far cry from my father's house, isn't it? But I've been very happy here, Philip—it was the best thing I could have done, to have moved away from Vancouver.'

He gazed at her in perplexity. 'You even look different. I don't understand it.'

Poor Philip . . . he was completely out of his element. Tucking her arm in his, she said, 'Come along, I'll make you something to drink.' They certainly couldn't sit on the rocks and talk, not with Philip dressed the way he was.

The unpretentious interior of her new home further reduced Philip to silence. He prowled around the room, peering out of the open windows where a cool breeze blew from the sea, picking up her books and putting them down again, examining her needlework, all as if looking for clues to this strangely altered girl he had found.

'Come and sit by the window,' Meg suggested, putting a plate of biscuits and two tall glasses of iced tea, decorated with slices of lemon, on the plain board table there.

He did as he was told. As Meg knew, Philip was an astute businessman used to the clawing competition of the executive world and well able to look after his own interests; he must have been severely shocked by her appearance and surroundings to have shown such a reaction. But now he had himself under control again. He took a long draught of the iced tea and then set down the glass with a certain deliberation. 'Your father and mother are celebrating their twenty-fifth wedding anniversary in ten days' time. They're having a big party, a formal dinner and dance. They want you to come home, Margaret.'

'All that way for a party?'

'Home for good.'

Involuntarily she shrank back in her chair. 'Oh, no—no, I couldn't do that.'

'It's where you belong.'

'Is it, Phil? Is it really?'

'Of course it is. It's where you were born, where you grew up, where all your friends are.'

She thought of Ben and Ada, of all of Ada's family with their unspoken loyalty to each other and their close ties, of Kevin, and of Paul and Chris. 'Not any more, Philip. I have friends here now. Better friends, I think, than those I had back in Vancouver.'

He looked her straight in the eye. 'Are you including me in that?'

'I have to, don't I, Philip?' she said quietly. 'After the accident you were yet another of my so-called friends who dumped me as if I had some unmentionable disease. You wanted to marry me before the accident, you certainly didn't afterwards. How do you think I felt about that?'

She felt a stirring of respect for him as he held her gaze. 'It's true what you say. I did stop seeing you—I thought it was the only thing to do. But after you left the west coast and came east, and you were no longer available, I knew I'd made a mistake. After your operation, if your father hadn't suggested I come and see you, I would have come anyway. Besides, I had a few days' vacation due to me.'

It was so typical of Philip to have all the arrangements dovetailing that she had a hard job to keep a straight face. However, any tendency to smile was removed by his next words.

'Your father and mother want you home. I want you

home. You could come back with me, Margaret. We could travel together.'

'No, Philip, I can't do that.'

'Why ever not?'

Briefly she paused to give thanks that Paul had come back to the island before Philip's arrival. 'Because I have a job here.'

He said sceptically, 'What kind of a job?'

'The little boy you met, Chris—I look after him through the day.'

'Come off it, Margaret—you mean you're just a glorified housekeeper?'

She raised her chin. 'I'm very fond of Chris.'

'And where does his father fit into all this?'

It was an effort to keep her voice casual. 'He's my employer, of course. So I can't go back to Vancouver.'

'Margaret, you're William Cairns' daughter—there's not the slightest need for you to have a job as a housekeeper. In fact, it's ridiculous!'

'You've got it wrong, Philip. On the island I'm not William Cairns' daughter—I'm Ben Cairns' granddaughter,' she retorted vehemently. 'A different thing altogether. Because for the first time in my life, I'm paying my own way. I've been doing needlework for a craft shop in the area, and now I have Paul's job. I'm independent, Philip—and you don't know how good that feels.'

The Philip who confronted her now was the Philip of the boardroom, used to pitting his wits against top-flight lawyers and company presidents. 'And how much is he paying you?'

She hesitated. 'We haven't actually discussed the amount. But I'm sure——'

'*I'm* sure it will be a pittance, Margaret. A mere fraction of what your father gives you as an allowance, for instance.'

'I daresay. But——'

'He's using you, surely you're intelligent enough to see that. You're here, you're available, and it's all very convenient for him.'

'It's also very convenient for me!' she retorted. 'And

you're missing the point, anyway, Philip. I don't *want* to go back to Vancouver—I like it here too much.' She leaned forward, gesturing with her hands to emphasise her sincerity. 'You see, I feel at home on the island in a way I never did in the house in Vancouver. It's as though a generation has been skipped. My father couldn't wait to leave here, whereas in a very real way I belong here.'

His pale eyes calculating, he said, 'That's all very fine and romantic-sounding, my dear, and even I can see that the place might have a certain appeal now, at the height of summer. But have you stopped to think what it will be like in February? You'll be totally isolated, cut off from any kind of social life——'

'February is a long time away,' she interrupted rudely.

Reflectively Philip stirred his drink, too wise in the ways of negotiating to persist in open confrontation. 'I must admit I wasn't prepared to find you so changed, Margaret.' He smiled at her ruefully, exerting all his charm. 'You're surely not so changed that you'll refuse to have dinner with me tonight?'

Had he phrased his invitation differently, she might have refused, for she knew Philip too well to think that he would give up easily. As it was, she said, 'I'd like that, Philip—as long as you don't spend the evening badgering me.'

'I promise not to.' He got up. 'I'll come for you around seven.'

Awkwardly she said, 'You have a place to stay, do you?'

'Of course.' He raised a sardonic eyebrow as he glanced at his watch. 'And now I'd better be going. We mustn't forget you're a working girl, must we?'

Before she could think of a suitable retort, he kissed her expertly on the lips, said, 'Until seven,' and left her alone in the room with, figuratively at least, her mouth hanging open.

She spent the rest of the afternoon with Chris, then went home to get ready for her date with Philip. Purposely she left her hair hanging loose and used a minimum of make-up, for it somehow seemed important to look as dif-

ferent from the Margaret of Vancouver days as possible;
fortunately the only long dress she had brought with her
was of very simple design, a pale pink crêpe with a square-
cut bodice and a slightly flared skirt falling from a high
waistline. She had just put it on and was struggling with
the zipper when a tap came at the door . . . he was early.

She managed to get the zipper all the way up, then
called, 'Hello, Philip.'

He walked in and stood for a moment in the open
doorway. 'You look lovely, Margaret,' he said.

There was open possessiveness in the way his eyes
roamed over her, and she shifted uncomfortably, wishing
with a sudden sharp irritation that he would call her Meg,
not Margaret. He had changed into a beige summer suit,
impeccably tailored; as always, his grooming was faultless.
There was no denying that he was extremely handsome—
neither was there any denying that he left her totally
unmoved.

He was walking towards her, a small florist's box in his
hand. 'Not knowing what colour your dress would be, I
had to play it safe.'

'Thank you, Philip,' she murmured. She had forgotten
about his almost compulsive habit of continuously
showering her with gifts, large and small; she had
grown to dislike it, for it had seemed to place her under
an obligation. She opened the box and found a single
perfect white orchid nestled in the tissue paper, and carefully lifted it out . . . she had never liked orchids. 'That
was very thoughtful of you.'

'Let me put it on for you.' Standing very close to her,
he pinned the corsage to her shoulder strap, his fingers
cool against her skin. She was suddenly and sharply
reminded of Paul, knowing that if his hands had been
brushing her flesh, she would not have been feeling anywhere near so calm and uncaring. Philip stood back to
admire his handiwork. 'There . . . are you ready?'

Meg picked up her long white shawl from the chair. 'I
think I have everything. Where are we going, Philip?'

'I'm staying at the Sea Winds Manor in Camden,' he
said, naming the most exclusive hotel along the coast. 'I've

reserved a table there for eight o'clock—that'll give us time for a drink first.'

They had been walking up the slope. Because Meg was gathering up her long skirt to avoid grass stains on it, she did not see Paul come out of Ada's. All she knew was that Philip had stopped in front of her, so that of necessity she had to stop too, to avoid walking right into him. He said huskily, 'You have no idea how wonderful it is for me to be with you again, darling,' and before she could elude him, he took her chin in his hands and was kissing her with a thoroughness and expertise that momentarily surprised her into submission. Just as her muscles began to tense in rejection, he released her, a gleam of triumph in his eyes, and forestalled any comment she might have made by saying, 'I know I shouldn't have done that, Margaret—I'll be on my best behaviour from now on.' He took her arm. 'Shall we go?'

It was only then that Meg saw Paul's tall figure standing by Ada's, and knew that he had seen everything. She said in a furious whisper, 'Did you do that on purpose?'

'What? Oh . . . there's your friend Paul.' His smile was charming, full of depreciation. 'It was a bit public, wasn't it? Sorry about that, darling.'

Paul was walking towards them. He was still wearing the shorts he had had on earlier but had added a white singlet, so tight-fitting as to be almost a second skin. Philip's sartorial perfection had left her unmoved; Paul's casual garments, far from new, left his tanned, smoothly muscled body to make its own statement. 'You're looking very elegant, Meg,' he said with deceptive lightness. 'I guess I'm out of the running tonight. I was going to invite you to come and look at a house with me this evening—give me the woman's viewpoint, as it were. But I gather Philip got his bid in first.'

His proposal conjured up an image of the two of them wandering from room to room, exchanging opinions, asking questions . . . almost as if they were a married couple, she thought, with a catch in her throat. 'Yes, Philip and I are going out for dinner,' she answered steadily.

'I see,' he said sardonically. 'You've got bigger fish to fry.'

Not one to resist a challenge, she looked him straight in the eye and said lightly, 'Not at all—you just didn't get to me soon enough.'

'You're right. I'm not used to having competition, am I?'

She knew him well enough to sense the anger under his repartee. It made her feel on edge, very much aware of him. Alive, she thought. Vibrantly, recklessly, wholly alive. 'We must be going,' she said smoothly, tucking her hand into Philip's arm and giving Paul a brilliant, provocative smile. 'Better luck next time.'

She saw the answering spark in his eyes, as blatantly he allowed his gaze to drop to the soft curve of her lips and linger there. He might just as well have kissed her, and there was nothing she could do to prevent the tide of colour that washed over her cheeks. She tugged at Philip's sleeve. 'Let's go, Philip.'

'Have a pleasant evening, both of you,' were Paul's final words, and as Meg and Philip walked away from him across the grass, Meg could feel, as palpable as a touch, his eyes following her. He had won that round, she thought, aware of a wholly deplorable urge to turn back and wave at him. Perhaps fortunately Philip spoke first. 'I think you should be very wary of that man,' he said soberly. 'He's a tough customer, Margaret, and I wouldn't want to see you hurt.'

'It's nice of you to be so concerned, but I think I'm quite capable of forming my own opinion of Paul Moreton, Philip—I'm twenty-two years old, after all, not seventeen, and besides, he's only my employer.' Her heels echoed on the wooden bridge. 'Do you see that bird flying over the trees over there? It's a great blue heron—a beautiful bird. You rarely see them actually in the cove, because the water's too deep. They go farther inland, into the inlets.' Deliberately she kept the conversation on an impersonal level as they got into the car and drove away from the island.

It was an evening in which all the ingredients were just

right. The girl in her long dress on the arm of her handsome, attentive escort. The magnificently appointed dining-room overlooking the sea. The exquisitely prepared food served by discreet waiters. Pleasant music from a small orchestra on the dais. And afterwards, a stroll in the velvet, star-spangled night, with the sighing of the sea in their ears, the scent of roses the final romantic touch.

But for Meg something was missing, and she was both astute enough and honest enough to know that the problem lay with Philip. He could not have been more courteous or charming; but although she tried to respond, it was an effort. She could hear her laugh becoming more brittle, her conversation more trivial, and with a shiver of revulsion recognised a reappearance of the old Margaret, that witty, shallow creature who had always been acting a part, hiding her real self behind a mask of gaiety.

She said abruptly, looking away from the restless black waters of the bay, 'Philip, let's go home. I'm tired.'

She missed his sharp, assessing glance. 'Of course,' he said agreeably. 'It's been selfish of me, keeping you out this late—I forgot you're a working woman now.'

There did not appear to be any sting to his words. 'Thanks—I *do* have to get up early. Chris thinks the best part of the day is before breakfast.'

They drove home making only desultory conversation, Meg by now longing for the evening to be over—she *was* tired, more tired than she had realised. However, when Philip left her at her doorway, she was able to say sincerely, 'Thank you, Philip, you looked after me very well.'

'My pleasure.' He smiled at her through the darkness. 'I'm afraid I won't be able to see you tomorrow. I'm making a few business contacts in Halifax in the morning, and your father wants me to have dinner with friends of his in the evening. But perhaps on Wednesday we could go out again?'

She had no real reason to refuse; and if she was only going to be here for a few days, another date could hardly cause a problem. 'There's a delightful little seafood restaurant about fifteen miles from here,' she suggested. 'Why don't we go there?'

'Fine. I'll pick you up at the same time as tonight.' He took her in his arms and kissed her, and she fought back a suffocating sense of panic. But once again he released her before she could pull away. 'Goodnight, darling. Pleasant dreams.' His light-suited figure strode away from her across the grass.

Exhaustion washed over her. She let herself indoors, feeling stale and oddly depressed. Not normally an untidy person, tonight she left her dress flung across the chair, her shoes by the bed, her lacy underwear on the floor. She couldn't find her nightgown under the pillow, so she tumbled into bed without it, wanting only to sleep and not wake up until it was another day . . .

Someone was shaking her by the shoulder. She burrowed her face further into the pillows. 'Go away, Chris,' she mumbled.

'It's not Chris, it's Paul. Wake up, Meg! I know you were late coming home last night, but I didn't know it was that late.'

It was Paul. She twisted free of his hand and half sat up, her hair tangled on her shoulders, her blue eyes still confused with sleep. 'What are you doing here?'

'Trying to wake you up. I did knock.'

She rubbed her eyes, then hurriedly pulled the sheet up to hide her breasts, colour scorching her face as she realised she was naked. 'What time is it? Did I oversleep?' she stammered.

'At least Philip left before morning.'

His voice was perfectly controlled, but there was no mistaking his meaning. Her chin snapped up. 'Philip didn't even come in last night.'

'Sure,' he sneered sarcastically. 'Who are you trying to kid?'

'He did not!'

'Then why are your clothes scattered all over the place and why are you sleeping without a stitch on?'

Her temper rose to meet his. Sitting up straight, still clutching the sheet, she retorted recklessly, 'What business is it of yours how I sleep—or with whom?'

'I'll show you.' He ripped the sheet from her fingers and flung himself across her, so that she fell back on the pillows. His hands were roaming her body at will, probing the softness of her breasts, smoothing her waist and hips, and her anger fled as a sweet ache-of desire flooded her whole being. In unconscious invitation her body surged to meet his, her hands that had been resisting him instead drawing him closer, her mouth opening to his kiss.

Then he was pushing her away, his face so distorted with self-contempt that she shrank back, her fingers fumbling to cover herself again. 'You've been with another man,' he said bitterly, 'and still I can't keep my hands off you.' He swung himself off the bed and went to stand by the window, staring out into the summer morning, his shoulders hunched.

She would not cry ... she would *not*. However, her voice did not sound quite her own when she spoke. 'I'm sure you didn't come down here just to tell me that.'

Paul's fist hit the window frame in an excess of frustration, and when he turned to face her, the same self-contempt was corroding his features. 'You're quite right, I didn't. I came to tell you about Ada. One look at you and that went clean out of my mind.'

'Ada? What about her?'

He hesitated as though choosing his words. 'She took a turn for the worse last night. We had to get the doctor a couple of hours ago. He's sending an ambulance—wants her in hospital where he can keep a closer eye on her.'

'Oh, Paul——' Her eyes were big with fear.

'Yeah ... it's not good. Pneumonia at her age——'

'Pneumonia?' she repeated, aghast. 'Ben must be out of his mind with worry!'

'He's going with her to the hospital. I'd better get back up there and see what's going on.'

'I'll get dressed and come right up.'

A curt nod, and Paul had left. Meg grabbed a pair of jeans and a knit shirt, and washed and dressed in record time. If anything happened to Ada, Ben would be heart-broken ... She left the shack, and the first thing she saw was the flashing red lights of the ambulance parked on the mainland; it must have come while she and Paul had been talking. As she hurried towards Ada's house, the door opened and two uniformed men carried out a metal-framed stretcher. Forgetting that she was still only supposed to walk, she broke into a run. Ben was as close to the stretcher as he could get, his weathered face uncharacteristically grim, while Paul and Chris followed behind, the little boy holding tightly to his father's hand.

Meg's eyes flew to Ada's face. A thick red wool blanket was pulled up to her chin, and the colour was reiterated by the hectic flush on her cheeks. Her breathing was shallow and rapid; her eyes were closed. Meg faltered, 'You'll phone us, Grandpa, as soon as you have any news?'

'Course I will, lassie.'

She had been walking alongside the stretcher. Now she fell behind, knowing there was nothing more Ben could say and nothing she herself could do to help. Her throat felt tight, and she hugged herself against the early morning chill.

Behind her Paul said matter-of-factly, 'Why don't you come and cook breakfast for us, Meg? Chris told me once you make fantastic scrambled eggs.'

She turned her back on the little cortège going across the bridge, with a shiver of superstition knowing she did not want to watch the ambulance drive away. Blinking away tears, she answered him, for Chris's sake trying to keep her voice just as calm. 'That's a good idea. Chris, you could help peel some oranges to have first.'

Paul put his free arm around her shoulders and the three of them went back to Ada's house. For Meg his gesture was easily explainable: he was grateful for her immediate support, that she had divined Chris's need for company. Perhaps there was even a modicum of comfort for herself in it, too. But it had nothing to do with the anger and passion that had flared between them such a short time ago. Nothing to do with love . . . as they entered the back door she managed to edge free of his arm, its weight too much a reminder of other, happier times.

The day passed slowly. Ben phoned to say Ada's condition appeared to have stabilised: while she was no better, neither was she any worse. In the evening Paul drove to the hospital to get Ben, while Meg put Chris to bed. When they arrived home, Ben was very tired and looked perceptibly older than he had a day or so ago. Obediently he ate everything Meg put in front of him, although the girl was quite sure he had no idea what he was eating. Then he sat in the rocking chair puffing on his pipe; he was going to spend the night in Ada's house, because she had a telephone and he did not.

Meg also was very tired. She kissed Ben goodnight and smiled guardedly at Paul. 'You'll call me if anything happens, won't you?'

'I will—goodnight, Meg.'

And that was that. Why had she somehow imagined him walking with her down the hill, perhaps even kissing her goodnight? She was a fool, she thought cynically; the only times he kissed her was when he wanted to make love to her. Philip kissed her because he wanted her money, Paul because he wanted her body. There was not much to choose between them ... neither one loved her for herself. In a thoroughly black mood, she went to bed.

CHAPTER TEN

THROUGH the night Ada had to have oxygen twice, but by midday the antibiotics appeared to be having an effect, lowering her temperature fractionally. Paul had driven Ben to the hospital first thing in the morning and then had come back to the island. In the afternoon, Chris accompanying them, he drove Meg in for a visit. However, she was only allowed to see Ada for a minute or two and found her frighteningly weak, so she spent most of the time with Ben, because she was worried about him, too. Because he couldn't remember whether or not he'd eaten lunch, she insisted on taking him to the cafeteria and sitting with him while he ate a sandwich and drank a cup of coffee. The minute he was finished he said, 'Must go back upstairs, Meg.'

'I'm sure she'll be all right, Grandpa,' she said gently.

'I know, I know,' he replied testily. 'That's what everyone says. I just feel better when I'm right there, that's all.'

Meg tried to imagine how she would feel if it were Paul lying so still in the narrow white bed, and knew she would feel very much as Ben did now; she took his arm in a wordless gesture of comfort as they went back up in the elevator.

Against her wishes, Ben had booked into a nearby motel for the night, wanting to be as close to the hospital as he could be. As Meg, Paul, and Chris got ready to leave, she said anxiously, 'You'll be sure and get some sleep tonight, won't you, Grandpa? It won't do anyone any good if you get ill, too—so don't stay up too late.'

'You're fussing over me like a mother hen,' he growled, but there was a twinkle in his eye, and she sensed he would heed her advice. She reached up and kissed his cheek, his beard rough on her chin. 'Phone us this evening.

And we'll come and see you and Ada tomorrow morning.'

He patted her awkwardly on the shoulder. 'Thanks, lass. Goodbye, Paul, Chris.'

The three of them drove back to the island. It was a little cooler there than at the hospital, but even so Meg was glad to get out of her dress and into a pair of shorts and her bikini top. She wandered up the hill to Ada's, feeling the grass tickle the soles of her feet, wishing she had thought to put her hair in a ponytail for coolness before she started to cook supper. Wishing, too, that she had a little more energy ... Chris was playing down at the shore by the bridge, for it was low tide, and she waved to him before going indoors, the screen door banging shut behind her.

Paul was scrubbing potatoes in the sink. 'I lit the barbecue,' he said. 'I thought we'd wrap the potatoes in foil and bake them in the coals, and then grill the steak. It means we'll be eating later than usual, but I don't think that matters. Would you like to make a salad?'

'That sounds a great idea—the barbecue, I mean. It's so hot, I didn't feel like cooking indoors.'

He gave her a quick glance. 'Why don't you sit down for a minute and I'll make you a drink. You look worn out.'

Meg smiled at him ruefully. 'Is it that bad?' He was standing very close to her, and because she was hot and tired and worried, she suddenly blurted, 'She will be all right, won't she, Paul?'

He put the paring knife down on the counter and wiped his hands on his shorts—all that he was wearing—before gently taking her by the shoulders. 'She's much improved over yesterday, Meg. And she's a fighter, you know that as well as I do.'

'I know,' she gulped. 'It's just that if anything happened to her, Ben would be lost.' Paul drew her closer and somehow she was standing in the curve of his arm, her forehead resting on his shoulder, and her predominant sensation was one of utter safety. 'He wants to marry her—but you know that.'

'You'd only have to be with them for five minutes to realise that.' He was stroking her hair, the movement of his hand repetitive and soothing. 'Try not to worry about her, Meg. She's in good hands, her family's all around, and Ben's right there.'

She looked up at him trustingly. 'You're absolutely right. Thanks, Paul, I feel better already.' Because of the closeness between them, a closeness she knew to be infinitely precious to her, she risked saying tentatively, 'Paul—about Philip. He didn't even come in to the house the other night. Honestly.'

She felt his body tense. Very slowly he said, 'All I could think when I saw your clothes scattered all over the place was that you'd made love with him—it nearly drove me crazy. But when I thought about it afterwards . . .' His eyes looked beyond her briefly. 'Because of—well, for various reasons, it's a difficult situation for me to deal with. But I do believe you. Meg. I really do.'

'I'm glad,' she said simply, knowing it was not the time to probe into those reasons, whatever they might be.

She could see from the expression in his eyes that he was going to kiss her, and it seemed absolutely right. Their lips met and clung in a kind of questing tenderness, a gentle searching, that for Meg at least was inexpressibly moving. She had lost all resistance by the time the kiss deepened, intensifying to more than a simple exchange of comfort and gratitude, instead expressing all the pent-up hungers of their bodies, their primitive need for each other. Her hands slid over his ribs to clasp the firmly muscled back and draw him close.

A shadow fell across the screen door, but neither of them noticed. Paul's hands were tangled in the heavy weight of her hair, caressing the nape of her neck; his mouth slid from her mouth to the fluttering pulse at the base of her throat, and from there to the valley between her breasts. She felt the trembling begin deep within her, and knew if his hands were to follow his mouth she would be lost . . . 'Paul, no,' she murmured. 'We mustn't. You promised you wouldn't . . .'

Light as gossamer his fingers drifted to her breasts, cupping them with infinite gentleness, and she moaned with pleasure. Deliberately he silenced her by kissing her again, his hands continuing their leisurely stroking. When he finally released her, his voice was blurred with desire. 'I know I promised, Meg. But it's a promise I can't keep—I must have been mad to make it. I want you so much . . . it's as natural to me as breathing.'

Want . . . but not love. 'You promised,' she repeated helplessly, shivering with delight as his fingers circled the tip of each breast.

'Then I'm taking it back.' Abruptly he clasped her by the shoulders, his eyes boring into hers. 'Let's start over again. Forget that I ever offered you a job—who the devil was I trying to fool, anyway? Marry me instead. Now. This week. To hell with reason and caution and good sense—what have they got to do with what happens between you and me every time we come within five feet of each other? Marry me, Meg—and I swear I'll do my best to make you happy.'

Hypnotised by the burning depths of his eyes, she swayed towards him, knowing she could fight him no longer. But before she could speak, the screen door squeaked on its hinges, and Philip's dry little cought came from behind them. 'Excuse me . . . am I interrupting something?'

With a muttered expletive Paul dropped his hands to his sides and swung to face the other man. 'Yes, you are,' he said in the same breath as Meg's faint, 'Philip—oh, heavens, I'd forgotten you were coming this evening.' With shaking fingers she pushed her hair back from her face, wondering what he had seen, how much he had heard. Was she relieved that he had arrived before she could commit herself to something she might afterwards regret? Or was she disappointed? She scarcely knew . . .

Philip looked disdainfully around Ada's cosy little kitchen before his gaze came back to travel over Meg's flushed face and scantily clad figure. 'I was under the impression we had a date tonight,' he said coldly. He drew back the sleeve of his light blue jacket to glance at his watch ostentatiously. 'Seven o'clock, didn't we say?'

Meg had recovered a little of her poise. Very conscious of Paul watching them both from his stance by the sink, she explained, 'Ada's been ill, Philip—she has pneumonia. She went into hospital yesterday morning and we went to visit her this afternoon. I'm afraid I've been so concerned about her that our date completely slipped my mind.'

'It hardly looked as though concern for Ada was uppermost in your mind a minute ago,' he replied in a clipped voice. 'However, we can discuss that later. Go and get changed—we'll still have time for dinner.'

He hadn't even asked how Ada was, Meg thought resentfully. 'Paul and I have already started to get a meal ready here. I'm sure there'd be enough for one more, wouldn't there, Paul?'

'By all means,' Paul said smoothly.

'So why don't you eat with us, Philip? I'd rather not leave the house for a while, because Ben said he'd phone around eight—that's when visiting hours are over.'

Philip's eyes flicked from one to the other of them. 'That's very kind of you both,' he said with patent insincerity. 'I accept with pleasure, Margaret—provided you'll at least come for a drive with me after your grandfather's phoned.'

Relieved that he had fallen in so easily with her wishes, she said rather more warmly than she'd intended, 'Of course. It's been so hot all day, a drive would be nice. Take off your jacket—you can help me with the salad.'

The food was delicious: fluffy baked potatoes served with sour cream, mushrooms and onions cooked in butter, tender, barbecued steak, and a crisp green salad, fresh from Ada's garden, tossed in her own herb dressing. Locally grown strawberries and whipped cream—of which Chris consumed an inordinate amount—and coffee for the adults, completed the meal. However, as a social occasion, it could not have been called an outstanding success. Paul and Philip, although outwardly polite to each other, reminded Meg of nothing more than two stray cats circling each other, looking for each other's weaknesses before attacking; Chris, overtired, made a fuss about getting ready for bed; while Meg herself craved nothing more than some time alone. She was already regretting her acceptance of Philip's invitation, although she didn't think she could possibly get out of it.

While they were clearing away the dishes, Ben telephoned, his tone cautiously optimistic. Ada had seemed brighter that evening, she had managed to eat a little solid food at suppertime, and she had ordered Ben off to the cafeteria to get something to eat himself. 'When she starts telling me what to do, then I know she's feeling better,' Ben chuckled.

'That's great news,' Meg replied warmly. 'And now I'm going to tell you what to do—you be sure to have a good early night and catch up on your rest.'

'Yes, ma'am,' Ben said meekly. 'A couple of Ada's boys are here, so we're going for a coffee first—is that okay?'

She laughed. 'Just be back by nine o'clock, that's all! Sleep well, and we'll see you tomorrow.' She handed the phone to Paul and started putting away the clean plates.

By the time Paul had rung off, the kitchen was restored to order. Even Ada would have approved, Meg was sure. Then she heard Philip say, 'If you're finished, Margaret, let's go down to your place so you can change. We might go back to the hotel and get a drink a little later on.'

Short of mortally offending him, she did not think she could get out of spending at least an hour or two with him. She gave Paul a bright, meaningless smile. 'I'll see you tomorrow. Don't forget your jacket, Philip.'

She started to turn away. But she should have known Paul better than to expect he would let them go that easily. 'By the way, Meg,' he said casually, 'you remember that conversation we were having before Philip arrived? Don't think it's finished, because it isn't. We'll continue it tomorrow.' He switched his attention to Philip, and for a moment his good-mannered mask slipped, revealing raw possessiveness, none the less genuine for being so transitory. 'And don't you get any ideas, Philip. You had your chance to marry Meg in Vancouver and you missed it— now it's my turn.' He gave them both a mocking salute, once again the civilised, urbane host. 'Have a pleasant evening.'

Meg took Philip's sleeve, preventing him from replying by steering him towards the door, feeling the muscles of his arm tight beneath her fingers as she said with a deliberate change of subject, 'Did your dinner go well last night?' The screen clicked shut behind them and they were out in the warm golden light of dusk. Unconsciously she relaxed, her eyes following the soaring flight of a gull over the roof of the fish shack.

'I scarcely think this is the time to discuss my dinner last night,' Philip said stiffly. 'Go and get changed. I'll wait for you in the car.'

Any number of retorts flicked through her mind. 'Are you sure you want to go for this drive?' she said with dangerous calm.

'Yes, I'm sure. You're not going to back out of that, too, are you?'

'Philip, I've already explained why I forgot about our date—I'm not going to do it again. Maybe we——'

'All right, I'm sorry, I shouldn't have said that. Let's go somewhere and have a drink. I think we could both do with one.' He patted her arm. 'I'll be in the car.'

Hurriedly Meg changed into a pale yellow sundress with a swirling circular skirt, draping her shawl over her shoulders. Her movements were automatic, for her mind kept returning to Paul's unexpected proposal of marriage and to her own damped down, yet simmering, excitement, that had, she realised, been with her ever since he had spoken. Maybe this time she would accept. Throw caution to the wind, as he himself had suggested. Marry Paul, live with him as his wife, share his bed . . . Impatiently she rubbed at her mouth, for she had smudged her lipstick. Brilliantly alive, her blue eyes gazed back at her from the mirror, daring her, challenging her.

Her hands stilled. What was she doing, going out with Philip now, when what she should be doing was walking back up the hill and telling Paul that she would marry him? Then, across the causeway, she heard the impatient summons of the horn, and knew Philip was waiting for her. It didn't really matter, after all, she thought. She would see Paul tomorrow morning. And that would give her the whole night to secretly savour the excitement of her decision . . .

A few moments later she slid into the seat beside Philip. 'Isn't it a gorgeous sunset? Look at those colours—should be another hot day tomorrow.'

He shifted the car in gear, his headlights picking out the gaunt, eroded rocks along the roadside. It was not so dark that she could not see his face; his lips a thin line, he said coldly, 'I thought when I first got here that there was more to this so-called job with Paul Moreton than meets the eye—and I was right.'

'Philip, do we have to talk about it?'

'We certainly do. Tonight he asked you to marry him, and I got the impression from the way he was talking that it wasn't the first time.'

Why did he have to sound so stuffy? 'You're quite right,' she said meekly. 'It was the fourth time, actually.'

'It's nothing to joke about, Margaret.'

'Well, you must admit you have to give him credit for persistence.'

'What I want to know is why you keep on refusing him.'

'Really, Philip, I don't think it's any of your business——'

'My dear Margaret, your parents sent me here to find out how you were and why you hadn't come home immediately after your operation——'

'I hope they paid your air fare,' she said silkily, her fingers clenched tightly in her lap.

She was pleased to see that, briefly at least, she had managed to disconcert him. 'That really need not concern you. The point is that when I get here I find you've let yourself get involved far too deeply with a man who's nothing but an adventurer.'

'You have no idea what Paul's like!' she answered hotly.

'As a journalist, you can be sure he knows every cent you're worth.'

Her fingers itched to slap his pompous, good-looking face; it was a good thing he was driving. 'Paul Moreton happens to be independently wealthy,' she said with admirable coolness. 'So you can forget the idea that he's after my money. He's far better off than you, for instance.' This was not very nice of her, for it had been well known among her circle in Vancouver that Philip Saunders lived beyond his means.

'Just what do you mean by that?' Philip demanded frigidly.

She was suddenly weary of the whole thing. 'Nothing. Let's drop the subject, shall we?'

The road had widened now, and unexpectedly Philip pulled off to one side and turned off the headlights. Staring straight ahead of him at the dying glow of the sun, he drummed his fingertips on the steering wheel as if trying to come to a decision. Finally he turned in his seat to face her. 'Margaret, I'm going to be completely honest with you.'

'I should hope so,' she murmured, but he was too intent on his own thoughts to pay her any heed.

'I've already told you that it was mostly to please your parents that I came east a couple of days ago. Oh, I'd thought about you through the spring and early summer, wondered how you were getting along, missed you—but I probably wouldn't have come to see you if your father hadn't asked me to. Then, when I arrived, you took my breath away. You were . . . different. You looked so much more casual and relaxed—and so very beautiful.'

Meg could not doubt his sincerity, although she was beginning to wonder what he was leading up to. 'That's kind of you, Philip,' she said. 'It just bears out what I've been telling you—that this place is good for me.'

'I don't know if it's just the place,' he said darkly. 'It didn't take me long to realise that Paul Moreton watches every move you make. Whatever his motivation may be, he's certainly after you.' He laughed humourlessly. 'What surprised me was how jealous I got. I couldn't stand it when he looked at you so possessively. And this evening when he was kissing you, I thought I'd go out of my mind. This visit has been an eye-opener for me, Margaret.

It's made me realise what I should have known six months ago—that I still love you.'

'Philip——'

'No, don't stop me now. I love you, Margaret—and I want you to marry me.'

She hesitated a fraction too long. He suddenly lunged at her and began kissing her: her cheeks, her hair, her neck, and finally her mouth. Her whole body shrank in revulsion, and had he but known it, that was his answer. But he must have mistaken her stillness, her passivity, for acceptance. His mouth grew more ardent, his hands fumbling for her breast, and she was shocked into action.

'Don't, Philip! Let go——'

'I won't hurt you, I promise. But you're so beautiful, and we'll be married within three months . . .' His voice was jerky, breathless; he had lost all his usual calculated suavity and charm. He thrust his hand into the bodice of her dress, and she pulled back in alarm. A button snapped off, falling into her lap.

Thoroughly outraged with him and beginning to get a bit frightened, she said sharply, 'Do stop, Philip! I won't have you mauling me about like this!'

'You always were kind of puritanical, weren't you? Different from the rest of the crowd—that's one of the reasons I was attracted to you in the first place.' He nuzzled her throat.

'That, and the fact that I had a very wealthy father.'

He pulled back, and she knew she had touched him on the raw. 'Okay,' he said thickly. 'So I was in a bit of a tight squeeze when I met you, and I did know there was money in your family—but that's not the reason I'm here now. I'm here because I love you and I want to marry you.'

'You're here because my father sent you—he couldn't even take the time to come and see how I was himself,' she retorted bitterly. 'Nor am I so naïve that I don't realise that both my parents think you're an ideal match for me.'

'So what if they do? Your father's grooming me to take the place in his company that his son would have had, if he'd had a son. Of course he wants you and me to get

married, it's only natural.' With a visible effort he lowered
his voice. 'But none of that alters the fact that I love you—
love you for yourself, not for what you represent.'

She scarcely knew whether he was telling the truth or
not; she did know she had never seen the phlegmatic,
sophisticated Philip so out of control. Perhaps she had
been misjudging him ... perhaps he did love her, after
all. Trying to be gentle and reasonable in an effort to
calm him down, she said, 'In one way, none of this really
matters, Philip. Because, you see, I don't love you. I'm
sorry—but I can't pretend to an emotion that I don't
feel.'

'Marry me anyway, darling,' he said urgently. 'Love
can be an over-used word, after all. We like each other,
we come from the same background, we have friends in
common. We could build a good life for each other.'

'No, Philip, I couldn't do that. And I'm not so sure we
do come from the same background any more—more and
more, this place feels like home to me, while Vancouver
seems farther and farther away. I rather doubt that I'll
ever go back except for visits.'

Silence ... a silence that stretched out uncomfortably,
so that in the end it was Meg who broke it. 'You could
surely have anticipated that,' she said. 'You've seen the
changes in me since I've come here.'

'Your father won't like it.'

'I can't live my whole life to suit my father. Let me be
frank with you, Philip—I've been a disappointment to
my father ever since I was born, because I wasn't the son
he'd been hoping for, the son who could take over the
little empire he was building. Ever since then he's seen
me as a pawn, someone to marry off to the right suitor.
I'm sorry to sound so Victorian, but I know that's the
way his mind operates. He doesn't love me. That doesn't
even enter into it. He only sees me in terms of usefulness.
So he'll be angry that I'm staying here and thwarting his
plans—but he won't be hurt. There's a very big difference.'

'Are you saying that you're planning to live here for
the rest of your life?' Philip said carefully.

'I don't know about the rest of my life—but certainly for a while to come.'

'I see.' He sat up a little straighter, and when he spoke the emotion was ironed from his voice. 'Your father suspected something of the sort might happen. He empowered me to tell you that he wants you back in Vancouver by the end of the month. If you don't come, he'll cut off your allowance.'

So the gloves were off . . . 'As I have a job, that won't matter, will it?' she said evenly. How typical of her father to think that by manipulating the purse strings he could manipulate her!

'A job! You can't tell me Paul Moreton will pay you anything near the allowance your father gives you.'

'Probably not. But then I don't need nearly as much money here as I did in Vancouver, do I?'

She could see him swallow, see him visibly relax the lines of his face. 'Margaret, we're getting off track—I didn't come to see you this evening to talk about your father, or money . . . I came because I love you, and want to marry you. Please, won't you reconsider?'

She could think of only one way to convince him. 'No, Philip, I can't. You heard Paul ask me to marry him tonight, didn't you? Well, this time I've decided to accept.'

'You can't do that! You don't know anything about the man.'

'I know the things that matter. That he's a good father. That he's intelligent and sensitive. That we laugh about the same things.'

'He doesn't love you the way I do.'

Not by even a flicker of her lashes did she show that his words had hit home. 'You have no way of knowing that,' she said shortly. 'Philip, why don't you just take me home? I don't think there's much point in us sitting and having a drink together—we really have nothing to say to each other.' His answer was to jerk the car into gear, and she felt a rush of relief—she had been afraid he might be difficult.

But her relief was shortlived, for instead of turning the

car around and heading back to Cairns Island, he set off in the opposite direction. 'You're going the wrong way, Philip.' He increased his speed and she added, hearing her voice rise despite herself, 'Philip, I want to go home.'

He had come to a crossroads where, with only a momentary hesitation, he took the right-hand fork. Meg felt the first touch of fear. 'This isn't the way to the island or the hotel.'

The needle of the speedometer rose steadily. 'I'm not taking you to the hotel.'

'Then where are we going?'

'You'll see.'

'Philip, this is ridiculous! Will you kindly turn around and take me home? I've had a long day and I'm tired.'

'You'll get home—but not until tomorrow morning.'

'What *are* you talking about?'

He negotiated a turn rather too fast, in a squealing of tyres. 'Well, it's this way, Margaret. You say you won't marry me because you're going to marry Paul Moreton. We'll see if he still wants to marry you after you stay out all night with me.'

Meg fought back a surge of panic. 'If this is your idea of a joke,' she said crisply, 'it's gone far enough—I'm not the slightest bit amused.'

'No joke, darling.' He glanced at her sideways. 'I'm a poor loser—you should remember that. If I can't have you, I'm going to make darn sure nobody else does.'

He slowed down slightly, as there was a fork in the road and he obviously wanted to read the green and white signpost. For a brief moment Meg contemplated opening the door and jumping out, but the impulse died quickly; he was driving far too fast for that. She would have to wait until they reached whatever destination he had in mind, and take her chances then. She said waspishly, 'No wonder you and my father get along so well—you're both living in the nineteenth century. You won't get away with this, you know, Philip.'

'With what?' Action had restored his customary suavity and now he sounded merely amused. 'Don't worry,

Margaret—I don't plan to rape you or hold you hostage—nothing as crude as that. You simply won't get back to Cairns Island until morning—that's all. Late enough in the morning that your friend Paul will see you come home and arrive at all the worst possible conclusions.'

With a sinking heart she knew Philip was probably right. Paul would assume she and Philip had spent the night together. All too clearly she could recall how swiftly he had suspected Philip of staying at her place a couple of nights ago, of how difficult it had been for him to trust in her word. Now, if she was gone all night, he'd be furious beyond reason.

She settled back in her seat, rather ostentatiously doing up her seat belt as the car whipped through the darkness. Too proud to beg Philip to abandon his plan—and almost sure it would be an exercise in futility anyway—she knew her only course of action was to wait, holding herself ready to seize the first chance for escape. All she needed was a telephone, so she could contact Paul and explain what was happening . . . she sat quietly, her hands folded in her lap, her whole attitude one of patient forbearance, while mentally she made note of the route they were taking, memorising the names of the little villages they passed through. She was almost sure she had never been this way before; she would have felt more at ease if they had kept to the shore road, for she and Paul had explored that thoroughly earlier in the summer. As it was she'd completely lost her sense of direction. What she did notice was that the villages were becoming more and more widely spaced, the houses more and more scattered. Neither observation increased her confidence.

Another crossroad. A left-hand turn this time, on to a dirt road. Ten minutes later a swing to the right down a noticeably narrower road which appeared to be completely uninhabited. At first she thought it was only a logging road, for there were long piles of trimmed tree-trunks lying along the embankments, and the headlights picked up the sawn-off brush and the mud trails in the woods left by the lumbermen: scenes of devastation that it would take years for the forest to repair. But then the cutting ceased, and dense woods took the place of the ruined forest. Overhead were curving limbs of spruce and pine and tangled branches of maple, while bracken grew to the ditches, a sylvan scene that ordinarily would have given Meg pleasure but now served only to emphasise the isolation and loneliness of their location. While the road itself was in good condition, having been recently graded, it was also progressively growing narrower.

About twenty minutes after turning on to the logging road, the woods opened up into a cleared area where a sprawling log cabin had been built on the shore of a lake. 'Here we are,' Philip said, with enough of a self-congratulatory note in his voice that Meg knew he must have been uneasy about finding the place. Before he switched off the car engine she took in as many details as she could, none of them very encouraging: no other vehicles, no lights, no telephone wires. However, the place must at times be inhabited, for there were well-kept lawns, a vegetable garden, even a few fruit trees, while a wharf jutted out into the waters of the lake.

Philip turned off the lights and the motor, taking the keys from the ignition and keeping them in his hand. 'Before we go in, let's get a couple of things straight,' he said. 'The car keys stay with me—this is the only set. The nearest telephone is back at the main road—exactly fourteen miles away, and I'm sure your doctor wouldn't want you walking that far. So you're stuck here until I choose to leave, which will be after breakfast tomorrow morning.'

She glared at him in impotent fury. He was right, she wouldn't even think of trying to walk fourteen miles. Nor did she think she could indulge in any kind of a struggle to gain possession of the car keys; it would not only be undignified, but futile. He had covered all the angles. She had no choice but to spend the night here ... damn, damn, damn!

'It was pure luck that I knew about this place,' he remarked. 'It belongs to the man with whom I had dinner last night—he offered it to me for the weekend, along with explicit directions how to get here. I didn't realise that I'd be using it quite this soon.'

'Congratulations,' she said tartly. 'You're wasted as an executive, Philip. The underworld is crying out for devious minds like yours.'

'Temper, temper, darling.' He stretched lazily. 'Let's go inside—I'll get you a drink.'

He got out of the car, locking the doors on his side and coming round to her door. Meg considered staying where she was, but the thought of spending the night alone in the car was less than appealing, so she got out, watching helplessly as he locked the other two doors, then following him up the path to the front door. Apart from their footsteps there was no other sound. Not a breath of wind disturbed the surface of the lake; the leaves hung still on the trees.

Philip unlocked the front door and fumbled for the lights. The place was very comfortable, furnished with a kind of rustic simplicity that was by no means cheap. But Meg was in no mood to admire the good taste or lack of it of the owners of the cabin; she pushed open the first door on the right, revealing a bedroom redolent with colonial furniture, quilts, hooked rugs on the quaintly uneven floorboards, and samplers on the wall. 'I'll sleep in here,' she announced, turning on the light switch which lit up three coyly imitational oil lamps. 'Goodnight.' Swiftly she latched the door in his face, glad to see a bolt which she slid into place.

'Margaret, you might as well be a good sport and at least have a drink——'

'No, thanks. You might put sleeping pills in it,' she said nastily. 'Goodnight, Philip.' She sensed him hesitate irresolutely, then heard his footsteps move away from the door.

Not allowing herself to think about her situation, for she was wise enough to know there was nothing could be done to alter it, Meg slipped off her dress and sandals and got into bed. The sheets smelled fresh and were newly laundered, and the bed was extremely comfortable. Having resolved to stay awake in case Philip should try anything, she was asleep in five minutes.

When Meg woke up, the first thing she saw was the quilt pulled up around her face. A totally unfamiliar quilt, its green and white patches neatly sewn by hand in rows of tiny stitches ... definitely not her quilt. Nor was it her room ... then she remembered Philip had brought her here last night. And now it was morning, and she would have to go home and face Paul.

She lay still. She had not bothered to draw the curtains last night, so that now the room was awash with the clear light of dawn. Outside she could hear a confused chorus of birdsong, and purposely she concentrated on it, trying to sort out the few calls that Ben had taught her to recognise: a robin, a chickadee, a white-throated sparrow. Somehow the naming of them brought her comfort; her eyes drifted shut and she slept again.

She awoke the second time to a more prosaic sound: Philip having a shower. It took only a split second for her brain to realise that this might be her chance. She got out of bed and pulled on her dress, then with infinite care slid back the bolt and undid the door. Philip had slept in the room opposite hers, for she could see the unmade bed through the open door. She hurried across the room. His trousers and jacket were draped over a chair, and with frantic haste she searched the pockets. A wallet, a handkerchief, some loose change, a comb—but no car keys. Nor were they on the dresser or the bedside table.

The water had stopped running. Too angry to bother disguising the sound of her steps, Meg went back to her room and finished dressing, carefully knotting the shawl across her breast to hide the missing button on her dress. Philip had finished in the bathroom; when he came to stand at her door, he was fully dressed, his damp hair slicked down. 'Good morning, Margaret. Did you sleep well?'

She too could play that game. 'Yes, I did, thank you. And you?'

He smiled at her. 'You didn't find the car keys in my room—too bad. Never mind, we'll be leaving shortly.'

'It can't be soon enough.'

'Oh, we must have some breakfast first—can't send you home hungry.'

The next hour seemed like one of the longest of Meg's life. Philip insisted on cooking bacon and eggs and toast and brewing a pot of coffee. She herself was both too impatient and too nervous to eat, and in the end she walked down to the wharf and sat down on it, hugging her knees as she watched the swallows dart and swoop over the surface of the water, their speed and grace only partly distracting her from the thoughts that circled in her brain. Round and round, all the various possibilities ... Paul would assume she had spent the night with Philip, had slept with him ... Paul would listen to her explanation and, knowing Philip, would believe it ... Paul would be too angry to listen to her at all ... as the minutes passed and the sun climbed slowly higher in the sky, she grew more and more frightened, her mood darkening as the day grew ever brighter and more beautiful. Throughout the summer she had had more than one opportunity to marry Paul. But now that she knew she loved him, and that her only chance of happiness lay in marrying him, it looked as though the opportunity was to be wrested from her—by, of all people, Philip. Philip, who loved getting his own way, who loved the ease and comfort and security that money brought, but who did not really love her at all. Paul *must* believe her, he must, he must ...

Across the lake, shattering its peace, echoed the blast of a car horn; Philip was obviously ready to leave. She scrambled to her feet and walked up to the cabin. He was sitting in the car waiting for her, and she slid into her seat without a word, her pale, set face discouraging any attempts at casual conversation. In complete silence they drove along the winding country roads until gradually their surroundings began to be more familiar to Meg and the dark green of forest on either side of the road gave way to the grey of rocks and the blue sheen of the sea. She glanced at her watch—nearly ten. There was no possible chance that Paul and Chris would still be sleeping.

Finally the car drew up by the bridge. The cove drowsed in the sunshine as still as a painting, each boat with its mirror image connected at the waterline. But the peace was deceptive. Even as Meg watched, she saw Paul come out of Ada's house and stand by the garden watching them. His hands in his pockets, he began to walk slowly towards the bridge.

Philip reached out and clasped Meg's wrist. 'I've done the best thing, I'm convinced of it, Margaret. Marrying Paul Moreton would be a step you'd regret for the rest of your life.'

'How very altruistic of you, Philip,' she said wearily, detaching his fingers from her wrist. 'You'll forgive me, I'm sure, if I say I never want to lay eyes on you again.'

'You feel that way now. But once this all settles down, you'll feel differently,' he said smugly. 'I'll probably drop by in a couple of days before I head west again. And I'll be willing to bet you'll be back in Vancouver within a month. Two at the most.'

For a nightmarish moment she wondered if he could be right—if two months from now she would look back on her stay on Cairns Island as a brief idyllic interlude, and on her relationship with Paul as the summer romance every girl should have as part of growing up. Would she be back in Vancouver as Margaret Cairns again, that brittle, insubstantial creature who seemed like a stranger to her now? She closed her eyes, breathing a quick prayer that Philip's prediction would be wrong. Then she got out of the car, knowing that she had nothing further to say to him. With an almost fatalistic calm she began to walk towards the bridge, and behind her heard Philip reverse and drive away.

CHAPTER ELEVEN

PAUL was waiting for Meg at the other side of the bridge. As she walked across the uneven boards, one hand resting lightly on the railing, her brain fastened on a number of unrelated images: a square-edged tear in the knee of his faded cords; the blinding whiteness of his singlet; a tiny abrasion on his chin where he must have cut himself while shaving; his utter stillness as he waited for her ... he too could have been a figure in a painting, she the silent observer.

She stepped off the bridge on to the grass. With no idea what she was going to say, she heard herself begin to speak. 'Paul, Philip kept me out all night on purpose, so that you'd think that he and I were lovers. He doesn't want you to marry me, you see.'

'And it just happened to be on the one night this summer that Ben hasn't been on the island?'

'Ben?' she repeated foolishly.

'Ben—your grandfather, remember?' he said with exaggerated patience. 'After all, you wouldn't want him knowing that you and Philip sleep together, would you? Ben thinks the sun rises and sets on you.'

'It's got nothing to do with Ben. I told you, Philip overheard you proposing to me. He doesn't want us to get married. So he kept me out all night.'

'Quite innocently.'

'Yes. We slept in separate rooms. He took me to a friend's cabin, miles from anywhere.'

'No telephone?'

He wasn't believing a word she said. She took a deep, steadying breath. 'No telephone. No neighbours. And too far for me to walk back.' Even to her own ears it sounded fabricated. What on earth could she say that would convince him?

'He just happened to know about the cabin, and it

just happened to be the night you knew Ben was away, and you just happened to tear that button from your dress.'

Her hand flew to her breast. 'Philip did that,' she said defensively.

'Now that's the first thing you've said that I believe.'

Her hand dropped to her side. The sun was shining right in her face, blindingly bright, yet unable to warm her or lighten her world. She should be fighting him, she thought numbly, presenting her case, arguing, anything. But something held her back, a vestige of pride that told her it was useless, he would never believe her anyway. Turning away from the sun and his impenetrable brown eyes, she almost tripped over a clump of grass.

'Where are you going?' Voice like a whiplash.

'To my place.'

'No, you're not. Ada wants to see you. I had to fob Ben off with the excuse that you'd got overtired and were sleeping in. Ben, being Ben, believed me.'

'You despise me, don't you?' Meg whispered.

Paul stepped closer, staying her with a hand at her elbow. 'Let me tell you how I feel,' he said very quietly. 'I decided to wait up for you last night—I wanted to see you again, because I had the feeling that at last you were weakening, that you were going to agree to marry me, and I didn't want to wait until morning to find that out. I didn't think you'd be late, you see. I got Chris off to bed and I worked for a while and before I knew it, it was going on midnight. And then it was one o'clock, and two o'clock, and still you hadn't come home. Finally by around three I'd convinced myself that you must have had an accident. I couldn't leave Chris and go looking for you, so I phoned the hospital and the police—no reports of any accidents. Only very gradually did it begin to dawn on me what you were really doing—staying out all night with Philip. Sleeping with him. It took me a while, because I'd come to believe you wouldn't do that kind of thing, Meg. I trusted you.'

'I didn't sleep with Philip the other night—you believed

me then. So why can't you believe me now? Nothing's changed. I'm still the same person.'

Impartial as a judge's, his eyes ran over her face. 'I don't think I know that person after all. I thought I did—but after last night, I find I don't.'

She had expected him to be angry, to shout, to hurl accusations at her, even to shake her bodily; what she had not expected was this icy calm, this dispassionate dissection of his feelings. Almost she would have preferred his anger. She could have fought it far more easily. But he was talking again . . .

'What I've had to come to grips with between three o'clock this morning and now is that I've made a drastic error in judgment. You're not as I thought you were, Meg. I could perhaps excuse you sleeping with Philip back in Vancouver—you were in love with him and thought you were going to marry him. But then he jilted you after the accident. What I can't understand is how you could pick up with him again as soon as he came back on the scene—don't you have any pride at all?'

It was plainly a rhetorical question. Meg waited, knowing there was more to come.

'The conclusion I've come to,' he went on heavily, 'is that Margaret Cairns is still very much alive—you never really threw her off. It's Meg who's the illusion. And it was Meg I was in love with.'

The world rocked under her feet. Her eyes huge in a face gone suddenly pale, she said faintly, 'What did you say?'

'That I was in love with you. I thought you'd have realised that.'

'You never said . . .'

'Don't you remember the day at the lighthouse? I was in love with you back then. Not that it really matters, does it?' Paul rubbed at his forehead and for the first time she saw the dark shadows under his eyes and the lines of fatigue around his mouth. If it weren't for Chris, I'd be leaving here today. But he exists—and he loves you. Uncritically. Wholeheartedly. So what the hell I'm going to do now, I have no idea.'

His words battered her like blows, his contempt like gall. At random she said, 'What does Ada want?'

'Oh, damn—I'd forgotten that. I'd better get Chris and we'll go.'

'But what does she want?'

'To see you, apparently—Ben says she's much better today. Wait here, I'm going to go and find Chris.' He strode away from her up the hill.

Everything seemed to be happening to Meg at a distance, and vaguely she decided she'd better go and change her dress. Her feet carried her towards the fish shack, her hands picked out a dress. She took off the yellow sundress, leaving it in a pale heap on the floor, and put on the green dress, the first one she had come across, doing up the buttons, the belt, flipping her hair over the collar. She looked around, wondering if there was anything else she needed, and decided there was not. Ada . . . she had to go and see Ada.

Paul had given Chris a small illustrated field guide to the seashore, and during the journey to the hospital Chris pointed out to Meg the shells, seaweeds, and starfishes that he had found, getting her to read the descriptive passages under the coloured pictures. She was grateful for his presence, for his chatter gave her time to collect herself, to regain a semblance of poise before facing Ada's needle-sharp eyes and Ben's subtler, but no less effective, discernment.

They left the car in the parking lot and walked across the pavement to the red brick building with its warm, stale hospital atmosphere that was such a far cry from the cool, salt winds of Cairns Island. Chris had tucked his hand into hers, and she knew that for him, as for her, these visits to Ada served to bring back memories of long days and nights spent in other hospitals far away, of discomfort and boredom and fear. Paul was presumably following them; it was more than she could do to look back over her shoulder to see. She had not looked at him directly since their conversation—to call it that for want of a better word—by the bridge.

She tapped on Ada's door, which was half-closed, and

heard her call, 'Come in, come in!' impatient and welcoming at the same time. Ushering Chris ahead of her, sensing Paul close behind her, Meg pushed open the door.

Ben was sitting close to the bed. He was holding Ada's hand, nor did he drop it when the three of them entered. He smiled at them, his blue eyes twinkling, the expression on his face a mingling of pride and happiness and lingering incredulity.

Ada was propped up against the pillows, her thick white hair neatly confined to its bun, her eyes unclouded by fever. Before Meg could say anything, Ada said briskly, 'Well, you'd better congratulate us.'

Although she had known instantly, from Ben's expression, what was going on, Meg was determined to make Ada actually say it. 'What for?' she queried innocently, not even looking at Ben.

'Tell them, Ben,' Ada ordered.

'Well now, why don't you tell them, Ada?' Ben replied, grinning widely.

'Humph!' she snorted, and Meg knew she was enjoying herself hugely. 'Your grandfather asked me to marry him once too often, Meg, and I've accepted him.'

Meg kissed both of them, hugging her grandfather fiercely, while Paul kissed Ada and shook Ben's hand, and Chris said in bewilderment, 'Will Ada be your grandmother now, Meg?'

'Well, sort of,' she temporised, laughing.

'And can we still stay on the island?'

No longer laughing, Meg looked up at Paul; it was her eyes that fell. 'For now at any rate,' Paul said lightly. 'And who knows, maybe we'll get invited to the wedding.'

'I should hope so,' Ben said gruffly. 'I'll need someone to help me get into my good suit.'

'When's it to be, Ada?' Meg asked.

'I'd like the banns read in church—so perhaps within the month.'

'Now that you've made up your mind, you're not wasting any time,' Meg teased.

The smile faded from Ada's wrinkled face. Her hand on the coverlet made a little movement and instantly Ben took it in his. 'No, dearie, I'm not,' Ada said soberly. 'It's years since I've been ill—it threw a real scare into me. Made me think. Life's an uncertain business and who knows how much time we have left. Lying here in bed, I decided I wanted to make the most of it—and that means marrying your grandfather.' She glanced down at their intertwined hands, Ben's so much larger, knotted and scarred, hers whiter, fragile-boned, the nails rounded and well kept. Her voice was so low when she spoke that Meg had to strain to catch the words. 'When I was so ill a couple of days ago, I knew Ben was close beside me all the time—and he was the one I wanted to be there. I needed him . . . that's when I realised that if I got better I was going to marry him—even if I had to ask him myself.'

Ben hit his knee with his free hand. 'I should have waited! Now if you had done the asking, Ada, I could have held that over you for the rest of our days.'

'I figured I could depend on you to bring the subject up,' Ada retorted.

Meg chuckled. 'I think you were quite safe, Ada. And you look so much better—getting engaged agrees with you. Have you told your children yet?'

'The two oldest are coming in this afternoon—I'm sure I don't know what they'll think.'

'They'll be delighted,' Meg said firmly. 'How much longer do you think you'll be in hospital?'

'Three days or so, the doctor thought. It'll be good to be home again. You're managing with the meals all right, are you, Meg? And have you watered my plants? And don't forget to keep the beans picked, they'll go tough otherwise, and to break off the dead pansies to keep the new ones coming. Maybe you should——'

'Whoa!' Ben interrupted. 'Meg'll do fine, Ada—you don't need to worry about a thing.' As Ada subsided with a meekness that amused Meg, Ben went on, 'But, Paul, there's something you could do for me if you would. I promised Randall I'd go fishing with him tomorrow morning—he's shorthanded. You wouldn't be able to go out with him instead, would you? I'd like to stay around here as much as I can, so I've booked into the motel for another night.'

'Provided Meg will look after Chris, there's no problem,' Paul replied smoothly.

Avoiding his eyes, she said, 'Of course I will.'

Because Ada was starting to look a little weary, the three of them left shortly afterwards. Paul bought them lunch at a restaurant in town, then they drove home. As they walked across the bridge, Paul said abruptly, 'Meg, could you take care of Chris for the rest of the day? I should go into Halifax—there are a few things I need to look up at a couple of the university libraries. I wouldn't be that late home. Around nine, perhaps.'

She nodded, smiling down at Chris. 'Sure, I'll be glad to.'

'The other thing is that I think you should sleep up at Ada's tonight. I'll be leaving the house around four in the morning to go out with Randall and I don't like to leave Chris alone.'

She stared at him in dismay, momentarily speechless. It was one thing to be under the same roof with Chris, quite another with his father. But before she could say anything, he interpreted her silence as consent. 'Thanks. I think Randall usually gets back in about ten or eleven.'

So that was that. In the next ten minutes Paul changed his clothes, gathered up his papers, and was on his way. From the front window Meg watched him go, her heart aching. Poets and romantic novelists might extol this emotion called love, she thought with a kind of desperate humour; to her it seemed a harbinger of dispute and pain and an unassuaged hunger. One man held her happiness in his hand—and that man believed her capable of lying and cheating, of sleeping with someone whom she didn't love . . .

'Meg!' Chris shrilled from the kitchen. 'Where are you? I want to find some more things from my book. Oh, there you are.'

He was so much like his father that tears burned her eyes. 'All right. Find your old sneakers and come and meet me down at the shack—I'll have to put on shorts.'

By deliberately blanking out all thoughts of Paul, concentrating instead on Ben and Ada's good news, on Chris's absorption in the bits and pieces he was collecting in his bucket, on the hot sun on her back, Meg got through the day. She and Chris barbecued hot dogs and boiled corn on the cob for their supper, a somewhat unorthodox meal which Chris approved of completely. By eight o'clock his eyelids were drooping, so she packed him off to bed, on his own request reading the section on crustaceans to him as his bedtime story. The anatomy of the crab, rendered in multi-coloured detail, was what finally sent him to sleep.

Meg went downstairs. She restored the kitchen to a standard of cleanliness Ada would have approved of, and then took out her needlework. She had been neglecting it lately, and she knew Kevin was anxious for more things from her, for he could sell as much as she could produce. The rhythmic movements of her needle in and out of the carefully stretched fabric should have been soothing; instead she found herself listening for every sound. The ticking of the old clock in the parlour. The gradually rising wind that blew the curtains into the room until she closed the windows, and that then rattled at the windowpanes, still trying to get in. The dripping of a tap in the bathroom.

It was nearer ten than nine when she heard footsteps on the back steps and heard the porch door open. 'Paul?'

He came into the kitchen, shedding his wet rain slicker and hanging it over the back of one of the chairs. 'You didn't need to wait up.'

'I wasn't,' she said coolly, not letting him see that his remark had hurt her. 'I'm way behind on Kevin's orders and I thought I'd try and catch up a bit.'

Paul was filling the kettle and putting it on the stove. Then he leaned back against the counter, watching her. As if the words were being dragged from him, he said,

'You look almost exactly as you did the first time I saw you.'

She looked up, the light behind her haloing her blonde hair, her eyes wide with enquiry, her lap filled with the brightly hued silks. 'Except I was in a wheelchair then,' she said gravely.

'Yes. Meg——' He stopped.

Carefully separating two threads of silk from the whole strand, noticing absently that her hands were not quite steady, she said, 'Yes?'

'The reason you wouldn't marry me all along—it was nothing to do with your inability to walk, was it? It was because you were still in love with Philip.' Not giving her time to answer, he went on, 'I can't get last night out of my mind. The only way I seem able to deal with it is if I can believe that at least you're in love with Philip . . .'

It was a temptation to lie, if only to remove the pleading from his eyes. 'No, Paul, I'm not. I suppose I was back in Vancouver—I'm not even sure now.' She put her embroidery hoop on the table beside her and stood up, walking over to him. With a nice touch of absurdity the kettle began to boil, its high-pitched whistle an assault on her nerves. Patiently she waited while Paul made the tea. Then, with a sense that she was fighting for her life, she said quietly, 'Please, Paul, can't you believe me? Last night was Philip's doing—he wanted to drive a wedge between you and me, and he's succeeded.'

Although he was gazing down at her, she had the feeling he was seeing not her, but someone else. And when he spoke, she knew her guess had been right. 'I've never told you very much about Annette—Chris's mother. You see, she made a habit of doing things like you did last night. She would go somewhere and be unaccountably delayed and phone me, always with a perfect excuse. She would plan to stay with a woman friend overnight, and months later I might find out that the woman friend hadn't even been there. At first, in the early days of our marriage, I used to believe her—I genuinely thought she'd had a flat tire, or had met up with a friend she hadn't seen for

years. Gullible, wasn't I? But the trouble with Annette
was that she wasn't a good liar—she wasn't clever enough.
She started tripping over herself, forgetting whatever story
she'd used the last time and inventing a new one. And
then, of course, the inevitable happened, and I saw her
with a man one day when she was supposed to be shop-
ping with Christine or Rose or Mary. And the whole
house of cards that our marriage had become came
tumbling down.'

Meg must have made some tiny gesture, for he said
flatly, 'Don't think I'm telling you this just to get your
sympathy. The point I'm trying to get across is that his-
tory is repeating itself. All those years ago, I thought I
was in love with Annette. And she'd look me straight in
the eye and lie her pretty little head off so she could be
with another man. She was always in love with her men,
you understand—each one was the undying and ultimate
passion of her life. Just as I was at one point, I suppose. I,
unfortunately, was foolish enough to marry her.'

'So you think I'm like Annette,' said Meg, stating the
obvious because she could not bear to hear the self-
contempt in his voice.

Paul drew his finger slowly round her chin. 'That's
right, my beautiful Margaret.'

'I'm not Margaret!' she lashed back. 'Nor am I
Annette. I'm Meg—and everything I've told you has been
the truth.'

'Can you take me to the cabin where Philip took you?'

She grimaced. 'I don't know. It was dark on the way
out there, and I'd never been that way before——'

'You sound just like her.'

'Because your wife was, by the sound of it, a patho-
logical liar, are all women liars?' she snapped, cut to the
quick by his comparison.

'I don't care about all women—only you.'

Unconsciously she rested her hand on his arm. 'Then
believe in me—that's all you have to do.'

He looked down at her fingers. They were tanned because she had been outdoors so much, and she had scraped
her knuckles today trying to free a barnacle from a rock

so that Chris could see what it was like underneath. 'You don't look like her,' he murmured. 'She has long finger-nails, usually painted a violent shade of red or pink, and she wears very ornate and expensive rings. Which fortun-ately Oliver has to provide for her now, rather than me.' In the same quiet, reflective tone of voice, he said, 'Have you slept with other men—besides Philip, I mean?'

'I've never slept with anyone!'

'Do you expect me to believe that? What about all the publicity about that beautiful socialite, Margaret Cairns? There wasn't much that was virginal about her.'

She said wearily, 'It was an act, and it served its pur-pose.'

'A damned good act.'

She shrugged. 'I suppose so. Although you said yourself once you could see the unhappiness under all the make-up and the glamour, remember?'

'So I did. One can be promiscuous and unhappy at the same time, though, I'm sure.'

'Promiscuous is just what I wasn't!' she said furiously. 'The rest of my crowd—my so-called friends—used to laugh at me and call me square because I didn't sleep around, like everybody else. Because I was that very old-fashioned phenomenon, a virgin.'

'You know, there's one way I could find out if you're telling the truth.'

Without any suspicion of what he meant, she said, 'Oh? How?'

Paul straightened, coming closer to her and running his hands lightly up and down her arms. 'It's obvious, isn't it? I could make love to you—I'd surely know then if I was the first or not.'

She pulled back. 'That's a despicable thing to say!'

His arms went hard around her waist, and without an undignified struggle she knew she was caught. As he bent his head and began kissing her, she held herself rigidly, fighting back her body's surging response. Against her mouth he said, 'Stop fighting it, Meg. You want this as much as I do.' With unexpected suddenness he shifted his grip and swung her up into his arms, carrying her across the kitchen towards the front bedroom.

Aware that Chris was sleeping above them and knowing how sounds carried in the old house, she hissed, 'Put me down, Paul! I hate it when you behave like this. Put me down!'

He dumped her on the bed and anchored her there by the wrists, his body hovering over her, his words punctuated by hard, angry kisses. 'I know you want me, Meg—all I have to do is kiss you to find that out. So you're fighting me for another reason, aren't you? Because you don't want me to find out the truth—that's it, isn't it?'

She writhed furiously in his grasp, her eyes blazing with rage. 'I don't care what you think about me any more,' she seethed. 'You might have divorced Annette two years ago, but you're certainly not free of her. And until you free yourself, you'll be no good to anyone else, Paul Moreton—you won't be able to trust anyone, or believe in them, or respect them.' Somehow she managed to get one wrist free, and she twisted sideways, half sitting up. 'Now get out of here, before you wake Chris up.'

He released her other wrist and she sat rubbing it, for his grip had been painfully tight. Light was streaming into the room from the kitchen, delineating his profile yet shadowing his eyes, so that she had no idea what he was thinking. He swung his legs around and got to his feet, his movements slow, almost awkward, and she said hesitantly, 'Paul, are you all right?'

He gave her an unreadable look. 'I'm going to bed. Goodnight, Meg.' He left the room, gently pulling the door shut behind him.

She sat on the bed until gradually her eyes grew accustomed to the darkness and she could discern the outlines of the furniture. Paul had already switched off the kitchen light and climbed the stairs to his room; she had heard the sounds of his steps moving around the room, then the creak of the bedsprings as he got into bed. Finding her overnight bag by the dressing-table, she changed into a nightgown and climbed into bed herself. For a long while she lay awake, wondering if she had been too cruel to have spoken so forthrightly to Paul about Annette, wishing that she had kept her conclusions to herself. Yet what else could she have done? Let him make love to her for the most cold-blooded of motives? Refused to defend herself? She shivered, feeling lonely and frightened, burying her face in the pillow to shut out the darkness and all the night-sounds of the old house.

Meg's sleep was shallow and restless. She heard the shrill of Paul's alarm clock, his quiet, almost furtive, movements as he came downstairs and let himself out of the back door. It was still dark, rain pattering on the window, and the wind sighing around the house. Some time later she heard the muffled roar of engines as the boats left the cove to go out to the open sea. It was daylight when she opened her eyes again, and a dull, grey day it must be, she thought, listening to the water gurgle in the gutters. It would be a good morning to show Chris how to mount some of his seaweed specimens. Maybe she'd make some bread, too, and fill the house with the rich yeasty odour of baking. She jumped out of bed and went to the window.

It could have been a day in autumn. A steady rain was falling, the kind that looked as though it would go on all day. It was windier than she had thought, for the spruce trees were bowing and swaying, and as she watched, a gull was driven swiftly across her field of vision. She felt a touch of unease at the thought of the tiny fishing boats heaving on the Atlantic swell, then resolutely quelled it; Randall was an experienced fisherman and would take no chances.

The morning went by rapidly. Chris arranged and rearranged his shell collection, then tried flattening out some seaweeds on old newspapers, while Meg kneaded the bread dough and made some cookies. Mid-morning she heard the porch door open, and called out gaily, 'Hi! Come in—you're just in time for an oatcake.'

But it was not Paul who came into the kitchen—it was Philip. The smile was wiped from her face. Without intentional rudeness she demanded, 'What are you doing here?'

'I told you I'd drop by before I left.'

So he had . . . conveniently she had forgotten it. 'When are you going?'

'Tomorrow. I came to see whether you'd changed your mind about going with me, or if not, if you had any messages for your parents.'

'You do pick your times,' she said bitterly, forgetting that Chris must be listening to every word. 'Paul's due back from fishing at any minute. When he finds you here, he'll jump to all the worst conclusions.' She glanced in the oven door and quickly removed the last tray of cookies. 'I'm not going with you, no. You can give my parents my love, and if you feel like it, you can tell my father I won't dance to his purse strings ever again. Now why don't you go, before Paul gets back?'

But she was too late. There was a clump of booted feet on the back step and she braced herself for the inevitable confrontation. But it was a stranger who came to the door, a short, red-faced man in dripping oilskins, his greying hair plastered to his forehead. Without preamble he said, 'Been an accident, missus. Okay if they bring them up here? We radioed ahead for the ambulance.'

'Yes, of course. But who . . .?' Meg couldn't finish the sentence, fear squeezing her throat shut.

'Dave Larrigan from South Point—his boat went on the rocks. And the feller who's been staying here—he was with Randall. He got him out. Here they come now.'

From this confused syntax Meg gained one clear message. Paul . . . Paul was hurt! She stood numbly by the stove, feeling Chris grab her hand and hold on tightly. She pulled him closer as two men awkwardly edged an old-fashioned wood and canvas stretcher into the room. Her eyes flew to the face of the man lying on it. A stranger, a young man with a new growth of beard, his eyes vacant and bloodshot, his face dead white; presumably Dave Larrigan. She indicated the front bedroom where she had slept last night, and they carried him through, depositing the stretcher carefully across the bed.

A second set of steps at the back door. Another similar stretcher, Randall MacKinnon holding one end. He nodded at her. 'He'll be okay—got himself knocked out. Put him on the couch?'

Chris was holding two of her fingers so tightly that he was hurting her. 'Yes, that would be fine,' she said faintly. Paul was covered with an old grey army blanket; his cheek was scraped raw, there was a swelling bruise on his forehead, and his eyes were shut, his lashes very dark against his skin. 'What happened, Randall?'

'Dave's boat went on to the rocks—damned young fool was out by himself in weather like this. Can't swim a stroke, of course. And his life-jacket was stowed away under the hatch. He broke his leg somehow when the boat hit and he fell overboard. Paul and I were the closest. I brought the boat in near as I could and Paul jumped in. Had a hell of a time getting Dave back to the boat. The rip tide's running and twice they almost went on the rocks themselves—that's how Paul got banged up. It was close, I'll tell you—close as I'd want to get. Dave Larrigan's a lucky guy. Wouldn't be here if it wasn't for Paul.'

Chris, who had been listening to all this wide-eyed, whispered, 'Is Dad going to be all right?'

'Yes, dear,' Meg answered, as much to convince herself as him. The two of them stepped closer to the stretcher. She could see now that Paul's hair and clothes were wet. Gently she laid her hand on his forehead, but although his skin felt clammy, it was not overly cold. He stirred very slightly, his lashes flickering, and she waited with bated breath to see if his eyes would open. But then he grew still again, his head falling sideways.

Randall and the other man had gone outside to see if the ambulance was coming; Meg had forgotten Philip's existence. She fell on her knees beside the couch, resting her forehead on the blanket, feeling the difficult tears of fear scorch her eyes. 'Chris, why don't you go up to your dad's room and bring down an extra blanket?' she suggested, not really wanting him to see her cry.

The little boy seemed glad to have something to do. As he ran upstairs, Meg let her tears trickle down her cheeks, knowing they were a reaction to those moments of sheer terror when she hadn't known whether Paul was alive or dead.

'You're in love with him, aren't you?'

She looked up, startled, 'Philip . . . I'm sorry, I'd forgotten you were here.'

'I noticed that—you love him, don't you?'

There seemed no point in evasion. 'Yes—I do.'

'So now you'll marry him and live happily ever after.'

'No, Philip, I won't be marrying him,' she said coldly. 'And that's your fault. You're the one who kept me out overnight, remember?'

'So it worked . . .'

'Oh, yes, it certainly did. You should be proud of yourself. He hates me now. He thinks you and I are lovers—and have been for years.'

Philip gave a short bark of laughter. 'That's rather funny—I'll have to tell him some time that I never got anywhere near you. Everyone in our crowd had you labelled as a real prude, but I suppose you know that.'

'I don't even care any more,' she said wearily. 'All I know is that you and your irresponsible meddling have ruined everything.' She heard Chris descending the stairs, dragging what sounded like a quilt behind him, and dropped her voice to a whisper. 'I would have married Paul if it hadn't been for you.'

When Chris came back, pulling the heaviest quilt he could find, she was on her feet by the stretcher, looking admirably calm. 'That's a good boy!' She spread it over Paul, seeing him stir again. Then the fishermen trooped back in and Randall said, 'Ambulance is here. I'll go in with them, and I'll give you a call as soon as I find anything out.'

'Thanks, Randall. Ben's at the hospital already, with Ada.'

'Right—I'd forgotten that. Maybe he can bring Paul home then.'

Randall's calm assumption that Paul would soon be home was comforting to Meg. From the front window she and Chris watched the little cavalcade go across the bridge, the men's jackets flapping in the wind. Then she said briskly, 'Lunch time, young man. And then right after lunch, we'll make some chocolate fudge—how would you like that?'

Philip cleared his throat; in the mélange of emotions that had claimed her as she had watched Paul's inert body being carried away, Meg had forgotten about him. It was the Philip of the boardroom and the business world who stood by the stove, very much on his dignity. He cleared his throat again and said pontifically, 'I must be going, Margaret. I have one or two matters to attend to before my flight leaves.' Distastefully he glanced down at Chris, and it was no problem for Meg to realise that he wished the boy was not there; she, however, had no intentions of tactfully getting rid of Chris, even for a few minutes.

'Goodbye, Philip,' she said evenly.

'Margaret, don't you——'

'Have a safe journey,' she interrupted ruthlessly. 'You can see yourself out, can't you?'

That she wanted nothing more from him was all too obvious. He said stiffly, 'Certainly. Goodbye.'

As she turned her attention to producing some sandwiches for lunch she heard the latch click shut and knew he was gone. Nor did she think he would be back. If only she could think of a way of undoing the damage he had done . . .

It was a couple of hours before the phone rang, time in which Meg kept herself and Chris as busy as possible. It was Ben on the line, and he had only good news for them. 'They'll be keeping Paul overnight just for observation, but the x-rays put him in the clear. I'll bring him home tomorrow morning, and in the meantime he sends his love. Ada'll be home the day after, the doctor thinks and all her crew, children and grandchildren, the whole works, think we should have got married at least five years ago.'

Meg laughed. 'I rather thought they might. You're staying there again tonight, are you?'

'Guess I will. If you don't mind?'

'We'll be fine.' Carefully she added, 'Tell Paul Chris and I send our love, too.'

Ben rang off, and Meg smiled down at Chris.

'Everything's fine. Your father will be home tomorrow morning, and he sends his love.' Had Paul meant that message only for Chris? she wondered. Perhaps he had . . . in which case she should scarcely have sent back the response she had. Oh well, it was too late now.

Knowing Ada would be home soon, Meg cleaned and dusted and polished for the rest of the day; in the morning she and Chris did some work in the garden, for the sun was out again and the air rich with the smell of damp earth and mulch and growing things. It was still quite early when Chris piped, 'Here come Dad and Ben!'

The truck had just come around the bend. Ben parked by the bridge, and he and Paul walked across and up the slope towards the pair in the garden. Meg was wearing a T-shirt and jeans, both shrunk and faded from many washings, and mud-caked rubber boots on her feet; she had tied her hair back in pigtails. In sudden panic she wished she had been waiting in the house, wearing her green dress and her high-heeled sandals and lots of make-up to give her courage.

'Dad—here I am!' Chris ran down the hill and flung himself at Paul's knees and in a flash of memory Meg remembered the pale, withdrawn little boy who had come here such a short time ago, a boy who would never have done what Chris had just done.

Paul had swung his son in his arms up over his shoulder. As he got closer, he said to Meg, 'Come here.'

She put down her trowel and walked between the rows of carrots to the edge of the garden, his image forever etched on her brain: dark hair ruffled by the sea breeze, scraped cheek, steady dark eyes and smiling mouth. A man's face, that was all . . . yet the one face that had the power to make her heart bang against her ribs and her mouth go dry.

'Closer than that,' he said.

Obediently she stepped nearer. Both his hands sup- porting his son, he bent his head and kissed her full on the mouth, then stepped back a pace. She gazed at him mutely, certain that he must hear the hammering of her heart.

With great interest Chris asked, 'Why'd you do that, Dad?'

'Because I wanted to.' He grinned at Meg, his teeth very white against his tanned face. 'That's a good enough reason, isn't it? Got time for a coffee break, Meg?'

'I—yes, of course,' she stammered, aware that she was blushing furiously, aware too of the three pairs of interested male eyes all observing her reaction. Belatedly she said, 'Hi, Grandpa—nice to have you home. How's Ada today?'

They proceeded to the house, drank their coffee, or, in Chris's case, juice, and cleared it away. Ben left to do a few chores at his house before going back to the hospital; Paul said, 'Why don't we go down to the shore for a while?'

'I'll bring my bucket,' Chris said promptly. He had not stirred more than two or three feet from his father's side since Paul had returned.

Over the boy's head, Paul smiled at Meg. 'Let's go.'

'I should finish the weeding before Ada gets back . . .'

'I'll help you with it later on.'

She could not resist him—yet what did he want of her? She followed him outside and Chris led the way to the shore. Meg sat on a rock, taking off her boots and rolling up the legs of her jeans, while Paul and Chris searched among the tide pools; Chris became totally absorbed in poking the sea anemones to make them close up tight, and then waiting for them to expand and start waving their tentacles again, so he could repeat the process. Paul climbed over the rocks towards Meg and sat down facing her. There was something about him, an air of suppressed excitement, that made her uneasy. She hugged her knees, waiting for him to speak.

'I'm going to risk asking you again,' he said quietly. 'This is only the fifth time, after all, isn't it? Meg, I want you to marry me. I love you, and I want you for my wife.'

Her eyes widened. Without even thinking about it, she opened her mouth to say yes. But then something stopped her—a need to have everything out in the open, nothing hidden or evaded. 'What about Philip?' she said evenly.

He nodded slowly, almost as if he had expected this response. 'I've done a lot of thinking about what you said about Annette. You were right—because she had lied to me so often, I was unable to believe in you. I thought the pattern was being repeated, that you were just another Annette, lying to me so you could sleep with another man. But out on the deck of that boat yesterday morning, and then when I was in the water not even sure I was going to make it back, I knew I'd been wrong—as wrong as I could be.' He took her hands in his, abstractedly rubbing her fingers. 'You're Meg, not Annette. You're honest and straight and kind, and I want you to be my wife.'

'Oh, Paul . . .'

'One more thing before you answer me. When they brought me up to Ada's on the stretcher, I kept drifting in and out of consciousness. I'd hear people talking and then it would fade away. But I can remember two things quite clearly—you saying you loved me. And Philip saying he never got anywhere near you. I grabbed on to both of those so tightly that right now I can hear the voices in my mind. Do you love me, Meg?'

Her eyes, the clear, unequivocal blue of the sky, were shining with happiness. He believed her . . . he trusted her . . . he loved her. 'Yes, Paul. I love you so much.'

Their kiss had all the surging power of the tides, all the sparkling beauty of the sea. He released her just long enough to say, urgently, 'I'm sorry I didn't believe you when you came back with Philip—God knows, I wanted to.'

Gently Meg touched his lips with her fingers. 'It's all right . . . I understand why you didn't and I know it won't happen again.'

He kissed her again and passion flared between them. He said exultantly, 'You're mine, Meg—I want you so much. And I'll want you until the day I die.'

The clatter of a bucket on the rocks made him break off. Chris had clambered up to them. Standing only a couple of feet away, he regarded them soberly.

Paul stretched out a hand. 'Come here, son. We want

you to be the first to know—Meg has agreed to marry me.' He broke off, looking at the girl in faint consternation. 'Actually, I don't think you did say you'd marry me—you will, won't you?'

She laughed. 'I wouldn't dare turn you down for the fifth time! Yes, I'll marry you.'

Paul squeezed her hand. 'So you see, Chris, Meg would live with us all the time. Would you like that?'

'Yeah . . .' he breathed, giving his gap-toothed grin. 'Will you let me keep my snails in the house, Meg?'

She tousled his hair. 'We'll have to negotiate that.'

Paul pulled her to her feet, taking Chris's hand in his other one. 'I think this calls for a celebration—let's all go out for lunch. And then we'll go to Halifax and I'll pick up a marriage licence—you don't want to wait, do you, Meg?'

His eyes lingered on her mouth, blatantly possessive, and she said breathlessly, 'No.'

He hugged her roughly. 'Neither do I.'

They climbed back on the grass and walked up to the house. Before they went indoors Paul looked down at the girl whose smooth blonde hair was blowing across his shoulder. 'This is what I want for the rest of my life,' he said in a low voice. 'You, walking by my side.'

She answered with all the honesty and love that was in her heart. 'I can't think of anything that could make me happier.'

'When are we going to eat?' said Chris.

Harlequin Plus

A WORD ABOUT THE AUTHOR

Born in England, Sandra Field today makes her home in
Nova Scotia, Canada. Converts, she says, are usually
fanatical in their new beliefs, and Sandra is strongly
attached to the Maritimes, with its sometimes inhospitable
climate but breathtakingly beautiful scenery.

She has lived in all three of Canada's Maritime prov-
inces, but it was during her stay on tiny Prince Edward
Island, where the beaches are legendary but the winters
long, that she decided to write a book. The local library
provided her with a guide for aspiring authors, and she
followed the instructions to a tee.

It was no simple job, she recalls now. In fact, a major
crisis occurred when she ran out of plot several thousand
words short of the mark! But a good friend coaxed her into
completing the manuscript for the simple reason that she
wanted to read it. The book was *To Trust My Love*
(Romance #1870), published in 1975.

Her many interests, which she likes to weave into her
stories, include birdwatching, studying wild flowers and
participating in such winter activities as snowshoeing and
cross-country skiing. She particularly enjoys classical
music, especially that of the Romantic period.

Legacy of
PASSION

BY CATHERINE KAY

A love story
begun long ago
comes full circle...

Venice, 1819: Contessa Allegra di Rienzi, young, innocent, unhappily married. She gave her love to Lord Byron—scandalous, irresistible English poet. Their brief, tempestuous affair left her with a shattered heart, a few poignant mementos—and a daughter he never knew about.

Boston, today: Allegra Brent, modern, independent, restless. She learned the secret of her great-great-great-grandmother and journeyed to Venice to find the di Rienzi heirs. There she met the handsome, cynical, blood-stirring Conte Renaldo di Rienzi, and like her ancestor before her, recklessly, hopelessly lost her heart.

Take these 4 best-selling novels FREE

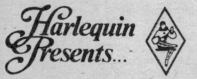

Your FREE gift includes

Anne Mather—Born out of Love
Violet Winspear—Time of the Temptress
Charlotte Lamb—Man's World
Sally Wentworth—Say Hello to Yesterday

FREE Gift Certificate
and subscription reservation

Mail this coupon today!

Harlequin Reader Service

In the U.S.A.
1440 South Priest Drive
Tempe, AZ 85281

In Canada
649 Ontario Street
Stratford, Ontario N5A 6W2

Please send me my 4 Harlequin Presents books free. Also, reserve a subscription to the 8 new Harlequin Presents novels published each month. Each month I will receive 8 new Presents novels at the low price of $1.75 each [*Total — $14.00 a month*]. There are no shipping and handling or any other hidden charges. I am free to cancel at any time, but even if I do, these first 4 books are still mine to keep absolutely FREE without any obligation. SB568

NAME _____ (PLEASE PRINT)

ADDRESS _____ APT. NO. _____

CITY _____

STATE/PROV. _____ ZIP/POSTAL CODE _____

Offer expires August 31, 1983

If price changes are necessary you will be notified.